Older Women need Love, too! Erika visits Atlanta

Dirk Caldwell Romantic Erotic Novels, Volume 5

Dirk Caldwell

Published by Dirk Caldwell, 2023.

OLDER WOMEN NEED LOVE, TOO! ERIKA VISITS ATLANTA

First edition. July 28, 2023.

Copyright © 2023 Dirk Caldwell.

ISBN: 979-8215523544

Written by Dirk Caldwell.

Also by Dirk Caldwell

Dirk Caldwell Romantic Erotic Novels
A Visit to the Farm with Darla - a Sexy Short Story
A Layover in Omaha with Tina
A Night in Eufaula with Lynn
A Trip to the Lake with Kim
Older Women need Love, too! Erika visits Atlanta
Lessons in Love: Gabriella visits Indianapolis
Big Girls Need Love, too! Barbara from Kokomo

Acknowledgment

Cover image by karlyukav on Freepik

Introduction

My name is Dirk. Well, that's not my real name. I'd never be able to have a normal life if I used my real name. I was an airline pilot and single at the time of this encounter. I enjoyed being unencumbered and the benefits that came from that. I could travel the world as an international aircrew member and be with any woman I wanted without regret and have always enjoyed the freedom that came with that ability.

I love women. I like them all, tall, short, fat, thin, old, or young. Attractive women and not-so-attractive are all the same to me. I specialize in dating women that are not getting enough attention due to their shape, size, appearance, age, or whatever. There are a lot of women that are underserved in that category. One of the few limits I put on choosing women was a lower age limit of 21, I'm no child molester. I had not experienced an upper limit as yet but have had sex with some ladies that were in their 50s and 60s that were a great lay. Most of the women in the unappreciated and underserved category I had sex with the most were horny as hell due to lack of attention and their behavior in bed showed that. Each woman was different, and I wanted to sample as many of them as possible before getting tied down. If I ever do get tied down.

I noticed that some women and I had a powerful sexual attraction for some reason. Maybe it was that they intuitively knew I would give them the attention they yearned for. I'm not sure why it happened, but for some reason, many women I've been with get very aggressive when it comes to sex, and many wanted to try new things. I was happy to help. I have a lot of repeat customers, and just as many that wanted sex once and were satisfied with that. Even after giving my usual disclaimer that I am not looking for a long-term relationship, I've had some close calls on emotional entanglement.

I enjoy recalling some of my favorite encounters. Most were great, some were just okay, and some I absolutely could not believe what happened. These are the encounters I write about, as they are the most entertaining and fun to read about. While most of the content in my stories is true, occasionally I do take artistic license and spice things up every now and then, but you would be surprised how much happened exactly as written. I've been incredibly lucky with women and am humbled every day that I have had so much success.

As a disclaimer, I always change enough of the information about the ladies so my writing could not possibly be traced back to them. Cities are changed, along with names, occupations, specific characteristics, branches of service for the military, etc. To do otherwise would not be gentlemanly. I do, however, mix in some of my local knowledge about locations. How did I get that information? Let your imagination be your guide.

I hope you enjoy my novels.

Wednesday - A Date That Did Not Work Out

I was looking at the menu board outside of the Cheesecake Factory in the fashionable Lenox Square shopping center in Atlanta, GA. After a disastrous first date with a woman that a friend had fixed me up with, my spirits were low, and I was seeking comfort. Maybe a piece of cheesecake or three would provide the needed emotional boost.

The woman had been nice enough, and very attractive, divorced, in her late 30s. When introduced by our mutual friends, there was not enough information exchanged to make an informed decision about whether or not she would be a good fit with my bachelor lifestyle. We met at a nice Italian casual dining place on the east side of the mall, and after some small talk and starting our first drink, things began to go south before the appetizer arrived. She explained that she had two school-age kids and told me unequivocally that she was looking for someone to be a Daddy for those and was ready to make a baby with a new husband. While I did not exactly recoil in horror, she could tell that I was not ready for that. I gently explained that I was not interested in a long-term relationship now or any time in the future. She finished her drink, said it was nice to have met me and left. I had a few bites of the appetizer, paid the check, and went outside into the warm Georgia night.

I heard my name called and turned around. My friend and fellow airline pilot Gina and her husband Matt were standing nearby with another woman.

"Dirk! How good to see you! What have you been up to?"

I had not seen Gina for a while. She was a Captain at my airline, and I had flown with her several times and really liked her and her husband. I even had them and their two boys out to my boat for a weekend one time. She had moved on to the Boeing 777 fleet, and I was still on the 767, so I rarely saw her anymore. We exchanged hugs, and I shook hands with Matt. They introduced me to the woman.

"Dirk, this is our friend Erika. We were neighbors when I was stationed up in Boston, and she is in town for a convention and looked us up."

I shook hands with Erika. She was looking me straight in the eye, for a little too long. Her handshake was dry and warm. She was dressed in a baggy polo shirt with the logo of some northeastern university, wearing baggy cargo pants, with sensible yet ugly walking shoes. She had a small backpack on her shoulder and no purse. Her hair was a short grey mop that looked like a bowl cut and needed a trim. Her face was lined and lean, with prominent crow's feet, round granny glasses, and some loose skin under her chin. About five feet seven inches tall, she carried herself with a good posture and stood calmly. She wore no makeup that I could tell, and her fingernails had no polish. Erika wore no jewelry that I could see except some small post-earrings. She wore a watch that was on the large side for a woman. I estimated her age at mid-60s. My mind automatically categorized her as a research scientist, nerd category 1.

Gina broke the silence. "We are helping Erika celebrate her birthday while she is here, so we are heading in for a dessert. Join us! We haven't seen you in forever!"

After a weak protest from me, they all coerced me into joining them. We went in and ordered drinks and a sumptuous dessert. The drinks came first. I told Erika, "Happy Birthday!" and we clinked glasses, and she smiled at me. She was looking at me closely, I wondered if I had something stuck to my face.

"I just turned 70," Erika said.

"Wow, congratulations! You sure don't look your age," I said gallantly. She kept smiling.

Gina explained further. "Erika is actually Doctor Erika; she is a tenured professor at a large university near Boston. She's also a psychologist."

I was impressed and changed my evaluation to academic nerd. "How cool, Erika. What do you teach?"

Erika explained she taught at the graduate school level, in the area of human sexuality and related subjects. "I also have a small practice where I see patients with a variety of issues."

Whenever I am around accomplished academics like Erika, I feel a little uncomfortable, like I am going to say something that will sound stupid, so I usually keep my mouth shut to remove temptation. She chatted about the Boston area and a bit about Gina and Matt as good neighbors. "Matt was always great about helping me with household issues, as I live alone and am not a good handyman."

In my head, the cogs clicked again, and I changed the evaluation to a single academic nerd.

Gina chimed in. "Dirk, tell Erika about your living arrangements." She looked at Erika with a grin. "He's the ultimate bachelor!"

I shot Gina a dark look. She was unremorseful. "Go on, Dirk, or I'll do it for you."

I took a deep breath as Matt suppressed a chuckle. "Well, Erika, what Gina is talking about is that I live on a houseboat on a nearby lake during the summer and have a condo in the suburbs for the winters."

Erika was fascinated and asked several questions about the boat, where it was docked, and other things.

Matt added, "He's always got a girl out there." It was Matt's turn to get my glare.

Erika laughed. "I'm sure Dirk has many guests, male and female."

I added, "Gina and Matt, along with their boys have been my guests out there. It's not a constant party."

We evolved into a pleasant conversation, with Gina and I managing to keep airline talk to a minimum for Matt and Erika. About a half hour later, Gina's cell phone rang. She looked at it, and said, "It's the neighbor. The boys are by themselves, I wonder what this is about?" She answered and went to the foyer so she could hear better.

We continued chatting among ourselves for a few minutes when Gina came back with a concerned look on her face. "One of the boys crashed his bike and is bleeding all over. The neighbor thinks he may need stitches." Matt and Gina traded concerned parent looks. "We picked up Erika from her hotel by the airport. Dirk ..."

I jumped in. I knew they lived in the opposite direction from the airport. "I'll be glad to give Doctor Erika a ride back. You guys run along and take care of your son."

Erika chimed in. "Thank you, Dirk. Gina, I'll be fine. I'm in town until Saturday, maybe we can meet up again."

Gina and Matt looked relieved and left quickly. Erika and I were by ourselves. She smiled at me.

"Dirk, I appreciate you offering to take me back to the hotel, but I can take a cab."

"Nonsense, I wouldn't dream of abandoning you. I'm glad to do it."

She smiled again. "Thank you, Dirk. You are a gentleman."

"Well, I don't know about that," I said modestly.

We finished our drink and dessert, and when the time was right, she said she was ready to leave.

Erika said she was at the Embassy Suites at the airport. I knew where that was, and we walked out to the parking lot. "Sorry, Erika. I forgot to mention I drive a pickup truck. Not the preferred mode of transportation for a college professor."

She laughed. "It will be fine. I've never ridden in one of these, it will be fun." She had a good sense of humor.

We headed out to navigate the highways of Atlanta and continued chatting. She had given a speech at her convention, so her part was winding down and it would just be a lot of meetings until she went home to Boston. Then she started asking more questions about my personal life, the usual about whether I had been married, did I have any steady girlfriends, etc. I answered those questions and told her about the miserable date I had that night, and she agreed that we did not sound compatible. Erika was easy to talk to, but I wondered if she was analyzing me as we drove.

The Proposal

We arrived at the hotel, and I was about to drop Erika at the door when she asked me to come in for a drink. "It's the least I can do after you drove me across town. Besides, I want to talk to you some more."

I wondered where this was headed but agreed. I dropped her at the entrance and parked the truck.

We went into the sparsely populated bar, and each ordered a glass of wine. The drinks had no sooner come when Erika started asking more questions. This time, it was very personal.

"Dirk, I'm doing some research for my practice and perhaps later on will fold the information I get into my classes on sexuality."

I thought, Uh oh! What have I gotten myself into?

She continued, "Can I ask you some questions about your sex life?"

I stammered, "Uh, Doc, I don't know if I feel comfortable talking about that with you. We've just met and ..."

"Dirk, I'm a practicing psychologist and hear this kind of thing all the time. It's mainly for my own understanding."

I felt embarrassed. "Well, okay. Fire away."

She smiled and patted my arm on the table. "How often do you have sex?"

I tried not to be flip and answer 'as often as possible.' "Ah, maybe two or three times a month."

"Are these experiences with different women or the same one?"

I tried to explain that it varied, Sometimes I came across a woman that wanted it once and that was it, and some I stayed with for days at a time. Some I dated several times at various intervals. It just varied a lot.

"I see. How do you meet the different women? Do they seek you out?"

Damn, she was straightforward. "Sometimes I just run across them, and sometimes they seek me out."

She nodded. "And how often do your sex partners achieve orgasm?"

I was stunned. "Well, a lot of the time. I have mostly very satisfied customers. Many of them have been kind of underappreciated so they are fairly ... enthusiastic."

"Very understandable. What is the age range of the women you have sex with? Do you prefer a certain age group?"

I was not sure where this was going, but I was starting to get a clue. "Probably from 25 to 65. I like more mature women; they are easier to talk to. I won't go any younger than 21."

She smiled. "That's quite an age range. What's the oldest woman you have had sex with?"

That was easy. "65, just a couple of months ago."

"Did that woman achieve orgasm?"

I thought back to Tina's very vocal orgasms and smiled to myself. "Most definitely."

She wanted more reassurance. "So, are you comfortable having sex with older women? Do their physical characteristics present any performance challenges?"

I was getting the idea. "Do you mean can I get an erection with older women that have bodies that reflect their age?"

"Right. Are you able to?"

I came right out and said what I was thinking. "Doc, are you doing research, or is this a job interview?"

She blushed, and a smile came across her face. "Dirk, normally I'm a very skilled interviewer, but I'm a little flustered and excited right now."

I asked gently, "Erika? What's got you flustered and excited?" I knew the answer already, but she had to say it out loud.

She stalled for a moment by taking a sip of her wine, then looked me in the eye. "Dirk, you are the reason I'm flustered. I find myself very strongly attracted to you on a physical, non-verbal, perhaps subliminal level."

"Does this mean you have a desire to have sex with me that you can't explain?"

She blushed again. "Yes, that's exactly it. I've never felt this before, and as a psychologist, I don't have an explanation."

I thought for a moment. "Erika, when was the last time you had sex?"

She had the answer ready. "Not for at least 10 years. I had a few ... affairs after my husband and I divorced about 20 years ago, but they were not fulfilling, and I sort of lost interest. While I had been curious about some sexual practices recently and was somewhat titillated, and when I met you, I felt a primeval urge to copulate."

I smiled at her college professor's terminology. I admitted to myself I was getting interested. "Doc, what do you have in mind?"

She tried not to blush again. "I'd like to conduct a field study by experiencing sex, seeing if a woman my age would enjoy it after a prolonged period of abstinence and be able to achieve an orgasm, and how a younger man interacts to achieve an erection to satisfy his older partner."

The Agreement

I looked her in the eye. "So, Erika. You are saying you want to do a study of contemporary sex practices, with yourself as an observer participating in a study, with me as the other participant."

"That's correct, Dirk."

"In other words, you are wanting to get laid after a long hiatus, with me providing the stud service."

"Also correct."

I shook my head. "I have never heard of such a thing! How many studies have the author participating in the study?"

Erika paused. "I'm sure it is not a common practice."

This was a unique conversation to be having in a hotel bar. I pondered all this to see if there was a downside. In front of me was a 70-year-old woman who was horny and wanted to explore sex practices. I was on days off from the airline, between girlfriends, and had plenty of time on my hands. I looked at Erika again.

She was in the underserved category where I liked to work. Plain, unadorned, and underloved, she was ready to renew her acquaintance with sex and it seemed interesting. While she was very different physically from the last ladies I had sex with, she seemed excited, willing, and eager, which went a long way toward enjoyment for both parties. Her study was so much bullshit, she just wanted me to fuck her. I was getting in the mood to do just that.

"Erika, I'm not looking for a relationship, short-term or long-term. There can't be any emotional complications after this. Actually, it sounds pretty straightforward. I provide a hard penis and you provide a vagina."

"I'm in agreement. Like I said, I'm attracted to you in a way I can't explain, and have wanted to have sex with you since about five minutes after we met. I have not felt that in a long time, the desire for a man to bed me, to be inside me. It's a fascinating condition and will be part of my study."

I thought for a minute. What the hell? Why not?

"Okay, Doc. I'll be your study partner."

She smiled. "Thanks! You will be providing a worthwhile service." She held out her wine glass and we clinked them together.

I had some questions. "How's your physical condition? Are you able to …"

"I'm good, Dirk. I had a hip replacement last year and a cortisone shot in the other less than a month ago. My gynecologist has me using a vaginal hormone cream that keeps that tissue supple and moist. I walk a lot, so my cardiovascular system is healthy. Physically, I'm sound for my age, well any age for that matter. My emotional state is sound, except for this current urge to have you rip my clothes off."

Doctors had their own way of speaking. I could not think of anything else to ask. "Well, okay then. I guess that's it."

Erika had a question for me. "Dirk, do you really think you can get an erection with a woman my age? I mean, my breasts droop, my stomach and buttocks sag, and I have age spots and wrinkles. I'm a realist. Young men like you are used to the more idealized image of a woman, thinner, firm, smooth, and perky."

"Erika, stimulation is a matter of attitude. With you projecting a sexual hunger like I am feeling from you right now, it should work. If it doesn't, I have my fingers and tongue. There are lots of ways to give you a solid sexual experience."

We had finished our wine. She looked at me with a shy smile. "Shall we go on up to my room?"

"I'm ready."

We walked to the elevator, and she selected the fourth floor. We rode up in silence, and when the doors opened, she found room 409 without any trouble and we entered. Standing just inside the door, it felt awkward for a minute, so I went to the couch and sat down. She went to the restroom and came out a short time later and went to the wet bar. There was a bottle of wine open, and she poured some for each of us into the elegant paper cups provided by the hotel. She sat down beside me. There was a brief moment of silence.

I asked, "Doc, I want to understand your needs. Do you want a quick roll in the hay, or something different? Are you thinking of a long, complete experience or something shorter? I've got all night, so it's up to you."

She looked thoughtful. "My first impulse is to get you inside me as soon as possible. But realistically, I would like to have you do foreplay of several different kinds, for my own personal satisfaction and data gathering, then do different forms of intercourse so I can see what my reaction is to those. Then in a perfect world, I would reach a climax as you do. That would hit all the points I am interested in. It's been a long time since I have had sex, so I am not sure all of that is possible."

I was formulating a plan. "Okay, Doc. I get it." I put my glass down. "Let's get you started by having you sit on my lap for a while and see how you feel."

She smiled shyly again and climbed onto my lap. "It's been a long time since I was this close to a man. I'm a little nervous."

"Don't worry, it'll be fine. If I am doing anything that you don't like, just call out 'Stop!' and I will." She nodded in agreement.

She was sitting on my lap like it was a visit to Santa Claus. "Take your glasses off, then go ahead and put your arms around my neck, that will feel more comfortable."

"Okay. Oh yes, that's better and feels more sensual."

"You can put your face into my neck if you want. I'm going to start caressing you, are you ready?"

I could feel her face nodding into my neck. I started slowly running my hands up and down her arms and legs outside her clothes, occasionally stroking her hair and neck. After a few minutes of that, I checked in with her.

"How's that?"

"It feels nice, comforting, and intimate, but without a lot of sexual energy."

It was time to see if she was serious. "I'm going to remove your shirt now. Hold up your arms."

She sat up and did as I had directed. Shirtless, I could see her sensible, plain bra. "Now you take my shirt off."

With the same shy smile, she tugged my shirt out of the waistband of my shorts and pulled it off over my head. She looked at my chest for a moment, then went back to nuzzling my neck. I touched her skin where her shirt had been, enjoying the feel of her back and sides. I ran a hand around to her tummy and made contact with her bare skin where it was available.

"Erika, you can caress me as well."

She nodded and began running her hand through my modest chest hair, and began exploring my chest, shoulders, and arms. Her other hand was tracing my neck and collarbones.

"How's that feel?"

She smiled. "Very satisfying, like the promise of things to come. I've been visualizing what your naked chest looks like. It's very sensuous to remove each other's clothes."

After a few minutes of light petting, it was time to move on. "I'm going to take your bra off now." She nodded again.

I reached back and with incredible luck, was able to unhook the bra one-handed. I eased the shoulder straps off her arms and tossed the bra on top of her shirt. If things went well, I'd have a pile of her clothing in a few minutes. Her boobs were bigger than I had thought. There were some stretch marks and they sagged down as expected. I took one into my hand and admired the heft and feel. Soft, warm, and meaty. Her nipples were pink and erect as I had expected. The areola was about the size of two quarters across and was dark. When I touched her boob, her breath caught a little.

"You okay, Doc?"

"Yes, very much so. I'm surprised that you touching my breast gave me such a thrill."

I smiled and caressed each of her boobs in turn, playing with the nipples and giving them some love. I alternated that with stroking her now naked back and running my hands over her belly. Her hands were busy running over my chest and arms. If she was going to stop me, it would be on the next step.

Committing to the Study

A few pleasant minutes later, it was time. "Okay, Doc. Let's get rid of the cargo pants. I'll take off your shoes and socks, then we'll slip those pants off you." She raised her head up and looked me in the eye.

"I'm ready." She was really going to go through with this, I thought to myself.

I started by unfastening her pants and belt. With them unzipped, I ran my hand around under her waistband to her panties for a minute. I then had to reach over and get the footwear and socks off her. "Stand up, please."

She stood in front of me, bracing herself with her hands on my shoulders. I slowly slipped the pants down her legs, as I leaned in and kissed her belly a few times. I ran my hands up and down the back of her bare thighs a few times, then slipped the pants the rest of the way down. Without me asking, she lifted each foot in turn, and the pants were off. She stood in front of me in just her panties.

"Panties, too?" she asked.

"Not yet." I intended to wait a while for those.

Looking up at her from my seated position, I told her, "We might as well do my shorts while you are up." She smiled again, so I stood up and she unfastened my shorts and belt, which fell to my ankles. I kicked them over to the pile of clothes as we both stood there in our underwear. She ran her hands over my back, and then down to my ass. I was pleased that she was interested.

"Let's sit back down and do more of the same."

Assuming the positions we were just in, we each had a lot of bare skin to explore. As we caressed each other, she couldn't help smiling and commenting.

"You're really good at this, Dirk. I would have never thought a man taking my pants off could be so erotic. I love how you are touching me all over without making it seem like groping. I'm enjoying this a lot!"

I love happy customers. I was running my hands up and down her thighs and stroking her breasts. After a few minutes of that, I started on her pussy, running a finger up and down her slit on the outside of the panties, tracing the labia. She caught her breath again as I touched her pussy lips. I continued that for a few minutes, then felt her tentatively tracing along the edge of my underwear. I took her hand and placed it on my cock, which was stirring. She got the idea and started running her fingers along the shape of it on the outside of the underwear. I stole a look at her face. She had her eyes closed, with a slight smile.

I leaned over and kissed her nipples for the first time, and she made a low moan as I did so. I circled each nipple a few times with my tongue, and then very gently nibbled each one. Feeling the time was right, I slipped a hand down into her panties. There I found that she had a very thick growth of pubic hair, surrounding her pussy and even the sides around the labia. I imagined it went from her panty line all the way to her asshole. Undaunted, I found the slit amongst all that hair and ran my finger up and down the labia, reaching the top and giving her clit an exploratory tickle. I was rewarded with a low moan.

"How are you doing?" I asked.

She gasped out, "This is very nice, I'm enjoying it!"

Without a word, I slipped her panties down to her ankles and left them there. Some women find that exciting. Then I gently spread her knees a little to open her legs and found her slit in all that hair. I inserted my finger gently in between the lips and slowly ran it up and down a bit before easing it into her vaginal vault for the first time. She responded with a low moan and started stroking my dick harder. I kept that up for a bit, then decided to try a test point.

"Erika, I'm going to have you sit on the couch." She opened her eyes and nodded, then slid over beside me. I moved the coffee table out of the way, and crouched between her legs, gently spreading her knees wide after I got rid of the panties. I looked her over.

Her lined face with no makeup was smiling, showing that she was enjoying the attention, and her erect nipples verified that. The boobs were sagging low over the tummy, and I could now see some stretch marks and cellulite on the belly and inside of the thighs. Her legs were firm, which must be because of the walking regimen. Her arms were a bit flabby on the back, and her hands showed veins and age spots. The bush was as I expected, totally surrounding her pussy, and was a wild, untamed thatch, mostly grey hair with some black. I had experienced that recently, so it was not a total shock.

I slid my hands along the inside of her thighs and parted the long pubic hair so I could see what I was doing. I ran my tongue along her slit north and south a few times, enjoying the sights and smells. There's nothing like the sharp anchovy smell of cunt, and the environment made me happy. She was moaning a little as I did this, then I pushed the tip of my tongue deep into her hole as she drew in her breath sharply. Her hips squirmed a bit as I did this, which told me her libido was waking up.

I licked her up and down for a while, then stood up, took her hand, and led her to the bed. I ducked into the bathroom for a washcloth to wipe my face. She lay on the bed, looking up at me with a smile. I lay next to her and began caressing her again.

She said, "That was wonderful. I'm putting that down as a very positive experience. We'll have to do that again."

With that, she sat up, pushed me onto my back, and took mysemi-rigidd cock into her mouth. I started to protest. "Ah, Doc. You don't have to do that ..."

She raised up, some saliva dripping from her mouth. She had a fist around my dick as she did so. "Nonsense, this is only fair to you, and I want to see how the stimulation works."

A guy can't argue with that logic. She proceeded with an enthusiastic pumping up and down. In the spirit of research and mentoring, I asked her to run her tongue around the shaft and the glans while she was there. She did as I had asked for a while and raised her head up again.

"That seems like it is getting a good reaction. Your cock got stiffer immediately."

I had to laugh. "Cock? Really, Professor?"

She was unabashed. "Of course. Using naughty language is very stimulating for both parties if neither is offended. Are you?"

I was still chuckling. "I'm good with naughty words, Doc. Stimulate away."

She gave me another minute of the enthusiastic and sloppy blow job, then lay back beside me, wiping her mouth on the washcloth. "What's next?"

I was already running my hand down her torso. "We'll move to manual digital stimulation of the vagina, with the goal of exciting the subject."

It was her turn to laugh. "Very well put. So, you are going to be fingering my pussy to get me hot."

"Precisely!"

She responded with some moans and sighs as I worked her pussy over with my finger. Each time I went deep into her hole and tickled upward, she wiggled her hips some more. She was ready to move on.

"Dirk? Can we move on to insertion? I'm wanting that badly."

I smiled. "Now, Doc, what would be the naughty language for that?"

"Shove your cock into my pussy!"

I looked up and saw her blushing with excitement. "Got it! Here we go."

Kneeling between her legs, I took two fingers and got some juice from her dripping pussy. The combination of oral sex and her hormone treatments had made her much wetter than I had imagined a 70-year-old woman would be. I applied the slippery love juice to the head of my dick and placed it in position at the labia. Her hand came down to guide my cock to the correct spot, and when things were lined up, I gave a gentle push with my hips and entered her.

With a gentle in and out motion, I went a little deeper each time, until after about four strokes I was all the way in, deep within her cunt. I could feel the head of my cock up against the end of the vaginal vault. I pushed against it gently for a moment, our pubic hair touching one another as our pelvic bones connected. A soft moan of, "Ahhhhhh!" escaped her lips. I held my position, getting her used to a dick inside her after a long absence.

I reveled in the moment. I closed my eyes and savored the experience. Pussy, there is nothing like it. Warm, wet, and slippery, enclosing my cock in a firm, smooth tunnel of pure ecstasy. I had my dick buried in a 70-year-old woman, and it was wonderful. I could feel my cock getting harder.

She said, "Oh Dirk! That feels wonderful. I've wanted that in me all night."

By way of answer, I reached to her boobs and caressed the nipples.

With a devilish look, she smiled up at me. "It appears that achieving an erection was not an issue."

"No, Doc, things are working well. It appears we have a very strong sexual attraction to each other. What would you like to do now?"

"Can you do it in some different positions so I can see what they are like? After we fuck like this for a while, that is," she said with that mischievous smile.

"Why, Doctor Erika! You are very good at that naughty talk!" She laughed and blushed a little.

I started a rhythmic thrusting into her, enjoying the feel. After a bit, she pushed back with her hips each time I went in. I loved it, this was so much better than a woman that just lay there and let me stroke away.

"Do you want to try it with you on top? A lot of women like that."

"Oh, yes please! I'd like to see what that's like."

I pulled out and lay on my back. She swung aboard me, straddling my hips with hers, taking a hand and guiding me into her again. Once she had the head of my dick in her, she looked a bit puzzled.

"Just lower yourself onto my cock, as fast or slow as you want until it is all the way in."

She responded by slowly impaling herself onto my rock-hard shaft until she was all the way down.

"Wow! That's in there really deep. Now what?"

"Now rock your hips forward and back, like you are trying to grind your clit against me. You can sit up straight or brace yourself by holding my arms or shoulders." She tried both ways.

She moaned a little. "This is a great data point. It's very stimulating and the woman is controlling the rate and depth of movement."

I chuckled again. Data point indeed. I started moving in and out of her, pushing up into her as she rocked against me while I played with her tits and nipples, which were swinging in my face.

"Ooooh, that's good, too! Great combination of different stimuli! It's very erotic." She exclaimed.

Then she said, "Everything is kind of sagging towards you. Is that a turn-off? I mean, I can feel my facial skin drooping, my boobs hanging down, and my belly against you. Is it unsightly?"

"It's more of the woman being self-conscious, I think. I've had women tell me to close my eyes during this part."

She nodded understanding. "I can see some women being self-conscious about their appearance to their partner during this. So, they just tell you to close your eyes and keep going?"

"Yes, sometimes, because it's a great position for the woman."

"Another good data point. I'm learning a lot."

I chuckled. "That's why we are doing this, for the data."

She had that mischievous smile again. "Well, that's one of the reasons."

We enjoyed this position for a couple of minutes. I explained, "This position is sometimes called cowgirl up, another way to say the woman is on top."

"Cowgirl like she is riding a horse?"

"Yep."

"Now I can see why so many of my patients enjoy riding a horse!"

I had always wondered that and now I was putting it together. "Want to try reverse cowgirl?"

"What's that?"

I explained, "The woman is on top, but facing away from the man."

"Hmm. Interesting. Sure, let's explore that. Do I just get off and turn around?"

I nodded. "As simple as that."

"Okay, here goes." She rose up, swung off me, turned around, and wiggled into position. This time, she took my cock in all at once and moaned again. "Ahhhh, that always feels so nice. So just start rocking like before?"

"Yes, Ma'am."

She started moving carefully, then faster. I reached around to her boobs and used a finger to rub her clit.

"Hmm. This is interesting. You can reach my pussy better, but it's harder to reach my boobs."

"Exactly. There are benefits and drawbacks. This is kind of a porn star move, it's a very naughty feeling but visually very hot."

"So, if a woman wants to fantasize about being a porn actor, she can do this?"

"Yes, and some women like it as well as regular cowgirl."

She thought for a minute while riding me. "How did you accumulate all this knowledge?"

It was my turn to blush; I was glad she was facing away from me. "On the job training, the Air Force was very big on that."

That got a laugh out of her. "While this is fun, I think I like regular cowgirl better than this. What's next on your training plan?"

"I think doggie style, where I do you from behind. Just dismount and get on your hands and knees facing away from me."

"Vaginally or anal?"

"Vaginally. We can do anal at another time if you want."

"I'm still deciding if I want to try that or not."

She dismounted and got in front of me, and I knelt behind her. She reached back and guided me to the correct hole. It's best to do this carefully, as sometimes a rapid, enthusiastic thrust will surprise both parties. She was so wet it was easy to slide my engorged cock deep into her. I pushed all the way in and waited, both enjoying the moment and giving her time to get used to it. I closed my eyes and enjoyed the sensation. I love doggie style and would have to be careful not to come while doing her.

She commented, "Every time you slide your cock in, it's the best feeling. Wow. Okay, do you enjoy this a lot?"

I admitted that this is one of my favorite positions.

She laughed. "Remind me to tell you the psychology of that during a rest break. Okay, do me."

I shook my head as I began thrusting gently into her. She was unlike any 70-year-old I had ever met. Instead of sitting in a rocking chair watching TV while crocheting, she had talked a stud into bed and was now encouraging me to fuck her doggie style. Amazing.

I fucked her gently for a while and reached around and played with her boobs, then asked how she was doing.

"Pretty well. I like it, but it is definitely not as stimulating as the cowgirl position. How is this for you?"

"It's really hot, I need to change to something else or I'll be coming soon."

"Sure, how do you want me now?"

"How about on your back again, this time I'll move your legs around and try a few more things." I pulled out, and she rolled over and spread her legs. I admired the view.

"By the way, that is a very erotic position. On your back, legs spread, inviting me in."

"It does feel very sexy!"

I moved to enter her and once again got a moan as I slid in. I put my hands behind her knees and started moving her legs up until her feet were straight behind me, and her thighs were vertical.

"This is a way to get deeper if the woman is wanting deeper and harder."

"I can feel that already."

I started pushing into her, and she moaned in response.

She gasped, "I can see why this is a favorite. I'm willing to try deeper and harder."

We did that for a minute, with her making appreciative noises.

"Want me to lift your legs higher?"

"Oh, yes please!"

I kept up deep thrusting as I lifted her legs higher and higher until I had her feet at my shoulder height. "How's that?"

She had trouble talking. "That's very good! Go ahead and do it harder!"

I did for a while, then lifted her ankles onto my shoulders and gave her some very deep thrusts.

She had an immediate reaction. "Damn! That's deep. It's good... keep doing it for a minute!"

I complied, then lowered her legs back down to a normal level. We were both sweating with exertion, but she was keeping up beautifully.

"Now wrap your legs around me and cross your ankles behind my back."

She did and started pushing against me. "This is great, I can push my pussy into you and get a wonderful feeling!" she gasped.

We pushed hard against each other for a minute, then I asked her to raise her legs and cross her ankles behind my neck if she could.

"I'll try, you can lift my legs for me ... oh, that's it! Wow! That is incredible! Pound me hard for a minute!"

My internal pressure had been building. "That's about all I can do, I'm about to come!"

She looked concerned all at once. "Oh Dirk, I'm sorry! I hadn't thought about that while you were showing me all the positions!" She unwrapped her legs from my neck and put them down, which helped a lot. "Go ahead and come!"

I said, "I'm not going to come inside you. I have the feeling I'll be doing some more oral later and don't want to make a mess of that sweet pussy of yours." I pulled out and got up on my knees. "Hand me that cloth, will you?" She did, and I aimed my throbbing dick at the cloth and started pumping it.

She surprised me by saying, "Here, I'll do that for you!" and put her hand on my slimy cock and started pumping. Then she pulled the cloth away, saying, "I want you to come on my boobs!" I didn't have much choice at that point. Then I had an idea.

"Let me put my dick between your boobs and I'll give you a titty fuck!"

She exclaimed, "Oh yeah, I've only read about that!" I scooted up and put my now very close-to-coming dick between her boobs.

"Push them together, around my cock." She did, and I started humping her tits. It felt heavenly. After about 30 seconds, I felt the pressure increase even more and groaned loudly as I exploded a jet of hot cum onto the base of her throat, followed by several lesser shots. She had released her boobs and with her hand aimed my dick at them, getting a good variety of streaks and dribbles onto her big titties.

I looked down at her chest, it was a mess. There was a puddle of cum at the base of her throat, dribbles and streaks of the stuff all over her boobs, and some on her breastbone. I asked her, "Why did you want me to come on you?"

She said matter of factly, "I had heard about it from patients and in some journals and wanted to experience it."

"Well, what do you think now that you have experienced it?"

She laughed, "I think it makes a mess for no good reason. I think men want to do it to show dominance over women by demeaning them. If women like it, the only reason would be to avoid pregnancy and keep their vagina clean. What do you think, do you like it?"

I thought for a second, which was odd since my now limp dick was still dribbling a little cum onto her. "I guess it's kind of kinky but did not think of it as demeaning until now. I can see that if the man insists on it. The times I've done it was at the request of the woman, like now. I guess I had better get off you and help you clean up. Let me get a damp cloth."

Cleanup and pillow talk

I went to the bathroom and ran the hot water until I had a warm, wet cloth. I went back and helped swab her clean. When she got all the major accumulation cleaned up we went to the bathroom and did a better job on her chest and neck, swabbed our pubic areas, then rinsed the cloths and hung them over the shower rail. We stood there naked, looking at each other. I was admiring her.

"Why are you looking at me with that smile?" she asked.

"I was just thinking there is nothing like a ... ah ... woman right after sex."

She smiled. "Dirk, what were you going to say using naughty words?"

"Well... there is nothing better looking than a freshly fucked woman."

Her smile widened. "Thanks. I like the way you look naked after sex as well."

"How about we return to the bed and cuddle while we think about the next steps."

"Good! The main thing my women patients want after sex is intimacy, like cuddling and kissing."

We got in bed, and I put an arm around her as she lay against my chest. I stroked her hair, back, and ass while she ran her hand over my chest and put her fingers through my hair. It was very pleasant.

She spoke after a few minutes. "That was a very pleasant and educational sex research session, but I am tired now. We were going at it for over an hour and a half!"

"I enjoyed it very much. Were you close to an orgasm?"

She sighed. "I loved the way things felt, sometimes very much, but it's not quite to the orgasm level."

I thought for a minute. "How about we take all the things that made you feel really hot, then we'll put them all together and see what happens?"

It was her turn to think. "That would be cuddling, caressing, licking, fingering, you on top, then me on top, then if needed you back on top with my legs around your neck while you are thrusting hard."

I smiled. "That's a damned fine list."

"Thanks! Dirk? How did I ... feel? Do I feel different than a younger woman?"

It was my turn to reflect. "Your textures are a little different, like your boobs are nice and soft, and your skin feels nice. I don't care about your tummy or butt that you say is sagging. Your vagina is in top condition. Whatever you are doing, don't stop. The feeling of it is fantastic. It's tight, smooth, and wet, much more than I expected. Some older women are a little dry, so we can just use some lubrication if needed. We did not need that at all for our first session, but we may use some later to make things really slippery and comfortable."

She smiled up at me. "That's a good analysis. Is my pussy really sweet? You said my pussy was sweet when were discussing where your semen was going to land."

"I meant it. It's sweet and wonderful."

She scooched up closer to me. "You keep talking about the next time. When will that be?"

"Hmmm. How about we talk for a while and then sleep a while, then see what happens? I can stay the night if you like."

She smiled up at me again. "I'd like that very much. What shall we sleep in? I usually sleep in a tee shirt and panties. What would you wear?"

"I can just sleep in my underwear and be okay."

We got ready for bed and resumed cuddling. She sighed with contentment.

"This is really nice, Dirk. It's a rarity to find a man that enjoys cuddling after sex, or anytime for that matter."

I shook my head. "I can't understand why more men don't like it. Who doesn't like lying next to a woman and feeling them close?"

She put on her psychologist's hat for a minute. "I think it's fear of intimacy and the possible emotional entanglements that may manifest as a part of that."

"I think you're right, Doc. This is about the time I repeat my spiel about no emotional ties and not mistaking lust for love."

She immediately got interested in that. "Have you had experience with that?"

"Oh, yeah! My failed marriage when I was young was a result of that. When the lust wore off, there was nothing left, and I had already tied the knot."

"Ouch! Does that still hurt, Dirk?"

"No, but I think that is why I don't want a long-term relationship. I don't want to get burned again. Even the thought of a short-term relationship scares me. I very recently have had very mixed feelings about a nice girl, but I don't want to confuse lust with love."

She thought for a minute. "When was this, Dirk?"

"Just recently, within a month."

"What's her name? Tell me about her."

So, lying in bed with a 70-year-old psychologist, I started telling Erika about Kim and how we had enjoyed our time together, but both had felt the beginnings of love which scared the hell out of me. Erika was easy to talk to, and I probably told her more about my relationships than I have anyone. I ended by saying we were taking some time off after a torrid week together and were getting ready to discuss the next steps.

"Thanks for listening, Erika. It feels better just talking it out."

"Anytime, Dirk."

I looked at my watch. "I've used up sleep time with talking. What's your schedule with the convention tomorrow?"

"Ah, I really don't have anything until after lunch. We can sleep in, or if we are not sleeping, stay in bed anyway." She said with a smile.

"I am in total agreement."

We turned the light out and spooned. She fell asleep almost at once, while I thought about the women in my life and what to do about them. After a while, I fell into a deep restorative sleep.

Thursday Morning – Try, try again

I could see the edges of daylight peeking around the curtains when I awoke. For a few minutes, I did not know where I was as I heard Erika using the bathroom. She came out and said good morning, and I took her place in the bathroom. I borrowed some of her toothpaste and brushed my teeth with my finger, then finger combed my hair and assessed my condition in the mirror. I felt good and rested, up for whatever was going to happen next. I went back to bed, where Erika was looking up at me, so I climbed back in. She came to me and started snuggling.

"Dirk, what other sexual things can we try before we work on my orgasm?"

"I have never heard such an opening line in my life!" I exclaimed.

She laughed. "I'm a woman on a mission. I need data."

I thought for a minute. "Well... there is light bondage, sex toys, anal, sixty-nine, some variations on the cowgirl bit... That's probably about it for our comfort level. "

"What's light bondage?"

"That's like tying your partner to the bed or using handcuffs to restrain them. It can be as simple as holding your arms down while doing you, so you can't get away."

She pondered that. "That's related to a fantasy of rape or conquest. Some patients really get off on that. I understand the sixty-nine but have never done it. Do women like that?"

"I think it's about 50/50. Usually, one person is ready to move on to something else while their partner is still busy with what they are doing. Some women find it kinky and risqué, so they just want to do it for a short time to check that box and move on."

"Okay, I want to try that for a bit. Sex toys?"

"Yeah, vibrators, dildos, ben-wa balls, all things that get inserted into various orifices. Some women like the vibrator applied to the clitoris while the dick is in them."

She laughed. "Do you have a vibrator in your back pocket?"

It was my turn to laugh. "No, usually the other party supplies that."

"Too bad. I wonder if they have them in the gift shop?"

"Hmmm. Should I call room service?"

She looked thoughtful. "I guess that would be the definition of a full-service hotel. Dirk? Can you please hang the Do not Disturb sign on the door before we begin?"

I smiled at her. "Are we going to begin?"

"Yes, indeed we are!"

I got up and made sure the proper sign was displayed and came back to snuggle some more. She still had her tee shirt and panties on, so I started caressing her under her shirt, playing with her boobs and nipples and sneaking a hand down her panties every now and then to run my fingers through her thick bush of pubic hair and run my finger along the labia. She put a hand on my cock and gently stroked it from outside the underwear. It felt nice.

She said, "I guess I should have trimmed my pubic hair. Do you find it unsightly or offensive? Should I shave it off like a lot of women are doing?"

"That's a very personal decision. Shaved pussies are all the rage now, I'm not sure why. Your hair is kind of long and surrounds your labia, and if it's a distraction to you then maybe do a trim or Brazilian wax. Sometimes it gets pulled into the vagina with the dick and can be painful for both of us. When it's wet I can just kind of push it out of the way, like this." I moved some stray hairs out of the way and slipped a finger up into the vaginal vault.

"Ooooh, that feels nice. You are advancing the agenda nicely. Is it wet enough?"

"I'm going to be licking it soon, so it will be very nicely lubricated before a cock finds its way in there."

She smiled. "Sounds nice. Don't forget the sixty-nine."

My cock was waking up. "No time like the present. But first I need to remove your clothing in a sensuous and sexy manner."

She laughed. "How do you do that with a tee shirt and panties?"

"By using my teeth only, no hands."

She smiled in anticipation. "I would have never thought of that."

"Sure, and that's how you will take my underwear off. Allow me to demonstrate."

I began the process of disrobing her, and as I did so we both were getting excited. I took her panties off and resumed lying next to her when she bent down and started pulling my briefs off with her teeth. "This is harder than it looks!"

She got the waistband down past my cock with some difficulty as it was growing larger. She kissed the end of my dick on the way down for good measure and soon we were both naked. Looking up at me, she said, "Okay! How does this work? Who gets on top?"

I said, "Most women like being on top for a couple of reasons. It allows them to move their head better, and an added benefit is that you don't have a pair of hairy balls hanging in your face."

She chuckled. "I can see the logic in that. Let's try it both ways since I'm gathering data."

"You're the customer. Lay down and we'll do me on top first."

She lay on her back, we wiggled into the correct orientation, and I spread her legs and buried my face in her pussy, and began licking up and down the slit, tickling the clit on each pass. She had put my dick in her mouth and was enthusiastically bobbing up and down on it, running her tongue around the shaft as she did so. After a couple of minutes, she wanted to shift positions. We did so, and I pulled her back into me and was rewarded with a face full of pussy. I put my tongue to work and was rewarded with some muffled moans from the other end. I heard a plop sound as she raised her head from my cock.

"This is much better for me. How is it for you?"

"I love this. It feels so cool having you basically sitting on my face with my tongue in you."

She laughed again. "I'm ready to lie back and watch you lick my pussy, driving me wild with desire."

She rolled off me and got on her back. I had her prop up on a couple of pillows behind her head so she could watch more easily. Then I got a pillow and put it under her ass to raise her up to a comfortable level for me. It's easier for me to get at everything I wanted, and it's kind of sexy for the woman. She responded, "Wow, that is sexy without you doing anything!"

I smiled up at her, then bent my head down and went to work. First, I spread her legs wide. This is pretty sexy by itself and gives me more room to work the pussy without getting her thighs sore from my beard stubble. I took a trip from south to north, giving the clit some attention. Women are different in how much pressure they like on the clit, so I was in experimental mode. I looked up at her and said, "Give me some feedback on how hard or how soft you want to me to work on you."

She was smiling already. "Kind of like a massage, like harder or not so hard?"

"Exactly!"

I rolled my tongue around her clit gently, then a little harder. I heard some moaning, then she whispered, "A little harder. Mmm, yes. That's just right."

Encouraged, I went down the inside of the lips, keeping hair out of the way, and stuck the end of my tongue into the hole of the vaginal vault. A soft moan came from above. I pushed deeper in and curled the tip up to get close to the elusive and mystical G spot. The feedback was immediate and positive.

"Oh! Oh! That feels good! Mmmmm." She gasped.

I went back to the north again and gave the clit some love, then repeated the deep dive into her hole. Each time, she moaned and groaned, indicating approval. After several minutes of this, I raised up and scooted up next to her, immediately sliding a finger into her now sopping wet pussy. She liked that a lot, and as I curled my finger up inside her, her hips squirmed as she moaned loudly.

Giving her clit a touch now and again, I caressed her boobs and nipples with my free hand as I laid her on her back and reached around. It's good to have long arms. She had a hand on my cock, pumping it frantically. Her squirming and moaning were nonstop now, and after several minutes of this very pleasant activity, I rose up, knelt between her legs, and slid my rock-hard shaft straight into her dripping cunt.

She cried out as I hit the bottom of her vaginal vault and began thrusting hard.

"Oh, oh, oh! Oh my!"

She was pumping her hips back at me each time I pounded her, and together we were making that hot sexy sound of flesh slapping together as we pushed against each other. I was feeling great, and she looked and sounded like she was digging it as well. After a few minutes, I sensed that she was not going to come like this, so I whispered into her ear, "Let's roll you over and you can fuck me!"

She nodded enthusiastically and as I pulled out and lay on my back, she rolled right on top of me and straddled my hips. She took my dripping cock and lined it up with the correct hole, then slid down on the shaft. She gasped as she took it all the way down. She braced herself on my shoulders and her hips started grinding against mine. I pushed hard into her each time she rocked forward. I found some boobs swaying in front of my face and caressed one while I sucked the other nipple. She groaned loudly with her eyes closed and worked her pussy against me feverishly.

I could tell she was pretty turned on and expected her to climax at any second. She kept rocking away, grinding those hips into me, as she bit her lower lip with a look of intense concentration. She was trying so hard to come. Sweat had broken out on our faces and was forming at the base of her neck and between her tits. After a few minutes of high intensity, she gasped out, "Get on top, Dirk! I want to try with my legs around your neck!"

She swung off me and lay on her back, panting as she did so. I mounted her at once and helped lift her legs up. She crossed her ankles behind my neck, and I started giving her pussy a pounding. She moaned and exclaimed constantly, with her hands on my ass pulling me deeper into her. This was as hot as it gets. After a few minutes, she said breathlessly, "I can't come. I want you to, deep in me. Come inside me, Dirk!"

I was not too far from exploding, so I kept up the position and speed, and soon my balls let loose a stream of hot cum deep within her as I groaned loudly in ecstasy. I lowered her legs and gently thrust for a few more minutes as spasm after spasm of my love juice shot into her. She was stroking my hair and back as I did so, in a very tender manner. I stopped and just lay there with my cock inside her.

She asked, "Can you roll us over with you still in me? I want to lay on top of you with your dick still in me."

"I can, but my cock is shrinking and may come out."

"I still want to do it. Please?"

I rolled us over while holding firmly onto her ass and managed to get into the requested position with my rapidly shrinking dick still in her.

She sighed contentedly. "Thanks, I just wanted to lie on top of you. It's very comforting. I also like the feel of your glans sliding out through the labia as it shrinks."

"I'm here to serve."

She giggled. It was the first time I had heard her do that. "That was really fun and felt great. I got close to an orgasm, but just could not get it to finish. What else can we do?"

"We are doing all the things you like, so in my esteemed opinion it will happen sooner or later."

She sighed and put her arms around my neck. "I feel like a big old dumb dowdy academic nerd trying to achieve an orgasm this late in life like it's critical to who I am. I am very content with my life and am really enjoying sex now, all thanks to you. Maybe I'm just too old."

"I don't think so, Erika. It'll happen if it's meant to be."

"That's very philosophical, Dirk. But I am leaving soon, and I may miss the opportunity."

We chatted about this and that, which was very pleasant with her lying on top of me. I had moved her legs down alongside mine, so her full weight was on me, and we were in contact from our chests down to our toes. I was gently stroking her back, ass, and upper legs. It was very intimate and enjoyable.

After a while, she asked if I wanted to talk about Kim some more.

After thinking a bit, I answered, "I think we have to see where that is going after some time. It can't be put off; it wouldn't be fair to Kim. But... there is a complication."

"What's that"

"Another friend of mine, who I was with just before I met Kim, wants to come out to the houseboat and hang out for a while."

She turned her face to mine. "What's this lucky girl's name?"

"That one is Tina and lives in Omaha," I told her all about Tina.

Erika shook her head. "How do you think Kim would feel if she was at the boat with you and someone slipped and told her about Tina being there?"

"Ouch. That would not be fair to Kim, would it?"

"Right. It sounds like Tina is just wanting more Dirk, not that I blame her. It probably doesn't matter where that takes place. So, meet her at another location."

I pondered that. "I think you have a point. Thanks, you're easy to talk with. I've never talked to a therapist, let alone in bed while I was stroking her naked ass."

She rose up and looked directly at me. "Dirk, it's not ethical for me to provide any real advice or direction because of our relationship. I can, however, listen as a friend and ask questions to help you find your own answers."

"I thank you, suitably chastened."

"Changing the subject, we should clean up and go down for breakfast. They do a great omelet that's included in the room charge. What time is it?"

I looked at my watch. "About 8 am."

She started crawling off me. "I'm all sticky, I need a shower."

"I'd be glad to share with you, in the interest of saving water," I said innocently.

"Offer accepted. Let's go."

Coming Clean

We went to the shower, adjusted the temperature after a brief discussion about the temperature, then took turns soaping each other. My policy is I wash the lady parts, the woman washes my man parts. I explained this, and Erika agreed. I had fun soaping her pussy, boobs, and legs. She was washing my front parts when I started getting a woody. She of course noticed and helped things along by washing it thoroughly.

She grinned. "Well, look what woke up. How long has it been since you had sex? Days, weeks, months?"

"Probably 30 minutes, we had a nice naked talk."

She admired my now rigid member, now bobbing a little. "You are one virile guy. What should we do about that?"

"I think if we towel off very carefully, it may not go off."

"Aww, that's not fair. You've been so patient with me."

She then surprised me by dropping to her knees and took my cock in her mouth and proceeded to give me a nice blow job as the water streamed over us and soaked her hair. After a few minutes of that very pleasurable activity, she stood up and turned the water off. "Let's towel off quickly and meet at the bed."

I did so in record time. She met me there but did not get in. Instead, she bent over the bed, with her ass turned to me. She braced herself on her elbows. "Here you go, Dirk. I know you like this position; this one is for you in appreciation for all you have done. Come and get it!"

A guy does not get an offer like that every day. I moved behind her, and as she guided my cock into her mass of damp pussy hair and found the correct hole. I pushed in right away and relished the feeling as I found the bottom of the vaginal vault. She made a contented sigh and said, "I just love it when you push all the way in."

I started a nice thrusting rhythm, and it felt so good I groaned with enjoyment. The feeling was great, and I started going faster. I reached around and found a tit and began fondling it and squeezing the nipple. She groaned in appreciation, so I used my other hand and started playing with her clit.

She was appreciative. "Oooooh! Harder, Dirk!"

Hearing that encouragement, I was invigorated and picked up the pace. I grasped her at the waist with both hands and pulled her into me with each deep thrust. Even braced, she was having trouble keeping her position until she was up against the bed frame. The bed frame was shaking and banging into the wall, I hoped her neighbor was not in the room. Her ass was jiggling each time I pounded into her, and her tits were swaying wildly with the motion. The super-hot sound of flesh slapping together started, and I knew I was in the zone. I was getting more and more wound up and was on the verge of coming. She read my mind.

"Let me know when you are about to come, we'll try and keep me clean inside."

I envisioned pulling out and coming on her back, or into a cloth. It turns out that was not in the plan.

I cried out, "I'm about to come!" The pressure was building in my balls.

She said, "Pull out!"

I did and was shocked when she spun around, went to her knees, and took my throbbing cock into her mouth.

"Erika ... I'm about to come!"

She wrapped her arms firmly around my legs, so I could not back away. There was a muffled sound that may have been, "I know!"

Then I could not hold back any longer and shot a load of hot cum into Erika's mouth as she bobbed her head back and forth, sucking every drop from me as jet after jet of cum came spurting out of my cock. I stood there with my knees shaking, as she gently caressed my ass and the back of my legs while rolling her tongue around the shaft of my dick and circling the glans to get every drop. After a minute, she pulled back and looked up at me with a smile and a little cum dripping out the corner of her mouth. "I've heard about that from my patients and wanted to see what it was like!"

I did not know what to say, so I helped her to her feet and handed her a cloth to wipe her mouth.

I said, "Wow, Erika! You are certainly doing some things I did not expect when I came up here last night."

She smiled. "With you, I feel like experimenting, I don't know what that's about."

"What was it like when I came in your mouth?"

"There is definitely an odd feeling as the semen gets in the mouth. I felt some icky sensations as the first wave splashed into the back of my throat. It's kind of slimy, but there is little taste. It was definitely erotic as I knew I was providing you with pleasure. What was it like for you?"

"It's a huge, kinky turn-on. There is something about looking down and seeing your head moving on my dick as I am coming. It's very exciting. Should you be taking notes?"

"Later. Let's get dressed and go down to breakfast. I'm starving."

We did, with me in the wrinkled clothes I had on yesterday, unshaven, and looking very sated. She put on a fresh baggy polo shirt and the same baggy cargo pants and walking shoes. We rode the elevator down to the restaurant in companionable silence and were eating when I marveled at the situation. There I was eating breakfast with a 70-year-old professorial academic nerd, with whom I had several hot rounds of sex with and who had sucked me off less than 15 minutes before. Looking at her in her nerd outfit with her mop of gray hair and granny glasses, nobody would ever suspect that she had the heart of a sexual tiger. She looked up and smiled.

"Dirk? You're looking at me in a funny way."

"I'm thinking our fellow diners would be amazed if they only knew what we had been doing just a short time ago."

She laughed. "Better keep that to ourselves."

Leaning over, I whispered, "Remember, there is nothing like the sight of a freshly fucked woman." Her eyes twinkled as she dimpled.

Dirk has an idea

I was finishing up when I had a thought. What if she got some nice clothes, did her hair differently, got a manicure and some makeup? Would she feel sexy and be able to complete her orgasm?

"Erika? Do you have to go to your convention today?"

She thought for a minute. "I have some meetings that I would just sit and listen at while trying to stay awake. I don't really have to go, I suppose. What did you have in mind?" She leaned closer with a smile and whispered, "Don't tell me you are horny again?"

"With you, it's a constant state. No, I was thinking you could take the day off and it will be my turn to experiment."

Her eyes flashed with excitement. "What do you have in mind?"

"I want you to have an orgasm, it's my goal for you. To do that, I want you to feel sexy. Some new clothes, maybe a new hairdo, you know. Girly stuff. Then I'll add romantic behavior to that to get you in the mood, and with you in the zone, try a few new things. I predict success."

"Are you going to spend the day with me doing that? Don't you have to go?"

I laughed. "I'm an unattached, single bachelor airline pilot on days off. Helping my friend achieve an orgasm while having some fun is what I live for. I'm happy to spend the day with you ... and even the night."

She smiled. "You staying with me for the day and night sounds wonderful, but I don't know about the other part. It sounds like a makeover."

"Well, in a way it is. A sexy makeover to stimulate the libido. Think of all the data you will gather about helping your patients have better sex. It will also support my theory that sex, lust, and romantic behavior lead to unjustified feelings of love."

I had her there. She grinned and said, "I agree with this experiment."

Smiling at her, I said, "Get out your credit card and hang on, Doc."

I stopped by the desk and got one of those complimentary packets of bathroom essentials, like a razor and shaving cream, toothbrush, toothpaste, etc. They looked at me funny when I requested two razors but handed them over. I was formulating a plan in my head and was thinking of a shopping list.

Back in her room, I shaved and cleaned up the best I could in my wrinkled clothes and day-old underwear. It would just have to do until I could get to a men's store. We sat on the sofa together and watched the news until the malls opened. She wrote out some notes on a laptop computer, and I turned my phone on for the first time.

I had messages from both Tina and Kim, both looking to set a date to get together. After getting some advice from Erika about how to handle the situation, I sent Tina a generic message on how I wanted to get together somewhere with her at a later date, and one to Kim that we should compare schedules when our new bids came out from the airline. Since Kim was a fellow airline pilot, she would understand the delay in coordinating schedules. I did not solve anything but was pushing the problem to a later date. It was still a mess.

Erika was looking at me. "Dirk, how do you feel about working on a schedule with those two women when you have been having sex with me and are obviously going to be having more?"

I squirmed a little. "With you, it feels like we are friends that like to have sex, what I call friends with benefits or fuck buddies. I guess it would feel a bit like cheating on a girlfriend except that they may not be real girlfriends. I admit it's odd. Is there any jealousy on your part?"

She thought for a minute. "No, I'm a realist and agree that we are friends having sex, which is really not all that unusual. I'm having a great time with you and am looking forward to more, but it's more than sex. I like you as a friend. When I leave, I'm not going to be sad, but very happy that we had this time together and will have some cherished memories and a new zeal for sex. I just don't want you or those two women to get hurt. I can tell you have some mixed emotions about them both."

With that, it seemed like a good time for a hug. We sat together quietly for a few minutes, then decided to get moving with our experiment. I did not have a good feel for where a big mall was on this side of Atlanta that would have everything I wanted, so I stopped at the hotel desk for some advice. They gave me some suggestions, and we got in my truck and headed out.

The Makeover

I decided to try the Greenbriar Mall on I-285 in southwest Atlanta. It sounded like they had everything I wanted. We entered, and I made a beeline for the mall directory. We were not too far from the hair salon, and after some discussion, made an appointment for a few hours from now. I then found a nail place and took her in there.

Erika had decided that it was my show, so I was doing all the coordination. Consulting with the Vietnamese ladies there, I ordered a manicure and pedicure. We all talked about the color of nail polish. Erika wanted clear polish, and I wanted more color. The nice lady helping us asked a few questions. I managed to convey the concept of date night, and she showed Erika a nice pale pink polish for her fingers, which she liked. I wanted redder polish for her toes, which Erika protested was unnecessary, but I had plans. I told the salon lady that she would be wearing white sandals, and she immediately got the idea and got the proper shade of red. Erika said, "I've never had a manicure or pedicure before!"

I sat beside Erika and got a manicure but with no polish. This place had cool massaging chairs to add to the ambiance, and the salon ladies brought me tea to sip on while Erika's work was in progress. I could tell Erika was having fun. We said goodbye to the salon ladies and walked out into the mall.

"Next stop, women's clothing." I steered my protege to a high-end store anchoring the mall and went to the women's wear section, where I engaged a nice saleslady.

"My friend Doctor Erika here is visiting us here in Atlanta. She is looking for a couple of nice outfits for some casual dates and then an outfit to wear for the trip home. What have you got in something with a younger, yet classy look?"

The saleslady went to work, and soon we were trying on nice blouses with patterns and matching those to skirts and shorts. Over her protests, I got Erika into a nice blouse with navy skirt, revealing nice legs with enough tan from her walking outside to be a great look. The size Erika picked was too baggy. I had the saleslady get her into a well-fitted size, that would hide her tummy but be snugger in the skirt. Erika protested.

"Dirk, the skirt is tighter than I like, and I don't even wear skirts!"

I was firm in my choices. She relented.

The next stop was the shoe department. I picked out some nice white open-toed sandals I had seen on my other girlfriends, and they had her size. It looked great with her new pedicure and cute painted nails. She admitted it was a good look. We left with the sandals in a bag, they would look goofy with her cargo pants. It was time to head back to the hair salon.

Our beautician was a whiz. She showed Erika a catalog, and we all liked a short, kind of spiky look that would be easy to care for away from the salon. For color, we gently talked Erika into a nice frosty silver with dark highlights instead of the mousy gray. The beautician went to work, and I left them with our purchases thus far and went to find a men's store, head back to the women's store, and then a variety store.

First, I went to a jeweler and got an inexpensive but nice necklace and earrings set. I had noticed Erika's ears were pierced, and she wore plain old post earrings. That would not do for date night.

The next stop was the men's store, where I found a couple of nice golf shirts on sale, and matched them with some sharp looking gray slacks, keeping in mind what Erika would be wearing tonight. I needed a few more nice shirts anyway, and gray slacks are always in style. Next were underwear and socks. I thought for a minute. The belt from my shorts would work, and my loafers would be okay. I was all set.

I went back to the women's clothing store and made a couple of purchases to surprise Erika with later. I was smiling as I left, they were as much for me as it was for her.

Now to the variety store. There, I bought a few supplies and headed back to the beauty salon. They were not done quite yet, so I hung out in the waiting area and read some old women's magazines.

After a while, Erika came out smiling. The hair transformation was a success, and the beautician had plucked and shaped the eyebrows as well. She looked ten years younger with the spiky silver hairdo with highlights.

"Dirk! I should have done this years ago!"

"Erika, you look great."

I then led her to the cosmetics section of the store I was at earlier. I had talked to a lady that applied makeup and gave lessons on how it was applied. She recognized me.

"Hello again! Here's your friend, please come sit down."

The nice lady gave Erika some makeup pointers and skillfully started applying some base, then blush, eye shadow, and eyeliner. When she was done, Erika was looking damned good. We picked out a conservative yet noticeable lipstick. I asked for some perfume samples, and we selected a very nice fragrance. Our work at the mall was done.

It was early afternoon. Makeovers take time. I asked Erika if she would like a chili dog for a late lunch, and she was intrigued. I took her to the famous Varsity restaurant over by Georgia Tech, an Atlanta favorite for many years. The ladies behind the counter yell out, "What'll ya have?" and then fill your order. We munched on our lunch and then I drove her through downtown Atlanta for a while before we headed back to the hotel to get ready for our evening.

We dropped our several bags of purchases and started thinking about getting ready. It was early yet, but Erika was excited, so I thought it was a good idea for the first of my surprises.

We had decided to shower separately to keep me under control, and she wanted to shave her legs since she would be wearing a skirt.

I said, "First, take off those cargo pants and get up on the bed."

She looked at me with a smile. "Is this pre-date sex?"

I had spread a bath towel out on the bed. "No, it's more grooming in preparation for the date. Get up on this towel and take your panties off."

She complied, with a quizzical look on her face.

I showed her a pair of sexy red panties I had gotten at the women's store. Her eyes widened.

"Oh Dirk, I could never ..."

"Oh yes you can and will, but first we will do some cleanup of the playground."

I pulled out a pair of inexpensive barber scissors I had bought at the variety store and got the extra razor from the bathroom.

"I am going to give your pretty bush a trim!"

She shook her head with a grin, "Dirk, this will be embarrassing."

"No, it will be erotic. This is all leading up to feeling sexy for tonight."

I laid her back on a few pillows so she could watch, and started trimming the hair from around her labia, and reducing the mass of hair to a manageable level. With the big pieces out of the way, I got a wet washcloth and some shaving cream and carefully shaved around the lips of the labia, and shaped the hair on her pelvis to a nice symmetrical shape. I compared the size of the sexy panties with the pubic hair and made an adjustment. It would not be sexy to have hair hanging over the top of the panties. During this time, I was handling her labia, and both she and I were getting a little turned on. After a final wipe to get stray hairs, I could not resist giving her a kiss on the clit, which made Erika giggle. Then she asked, "How about a quickie before my shower? I'm a little worked up."

I laughed, "Doctor Erika! I'm surprised at you. I've made you into a horny woman! Wait for tonight, this is all part of the buildup."

She did not have a shower cap to protect her hair during the shower, so I went back to my variety store bag and pulled one out.

"Dirk, you have thought of everything!"

"Try not to get your face wet to save your makeup, and here is a small tin of Vaseline to put on the area around your labia where I shaved you, it will help with any irritation. Now get in the shower by yourself before I decide to stick this boner in you! And here is some good smelling bath soap, that hotel soap sucks."

I swatted her naked ass and sent her into the shower, feeling virtuous. Shaving her pussy had really turned me on.

She came out after a bit with a towel wrapped around her, and I directed her to the sofa, where I had a bath towel spread out. "Sit here with your new panties on, I got you some sunless tanning lotion for your legs." She looked at me in amazement.

"Hey, it'll make your legs look even better, and be sure to do your feet. Your white sandals and pedicure will really pop with a little tan. It takes about 30 minutes to dry, so hang out here until it's time to get dressed. I'll help with that."

She was shaking your head. "Dirk, you are really good at this. How did you ... Never mind."

"The adventure continues. Do you want to press your blouse or skirt? I'm going to iron my new golf shirt and slacks so they will look sharp."

"Just get the iron and board out and I'll do them while my legs are drying."

"Thanks. I'm going to shower and shave now. By myself, my heart will be breaking from loneliness."

She was not affected by my display and sat down to start applying the tanning lotion. By the time I got out of the shower, she had my clothes pressed and was working on hers, wearing just her old bra and the new red panties.

I had another surprise. Going to my bag of purchases, I pulled out a sexy red push-up bra that I had gotten earlier. "That old white bra does not go with those sexy panties."

She looked at me in surprise. I said, "Let me help you with changing into the new one," and went to her and removed the old plain white bra, and helped her into the new one, sneaking a feel of her boobs as I did so.

"Dirk, it fits great, how did you know my size?"

"I looked at the label of your old one. Go look at yourself in the mirror."

She did and turned back and forth to admire the look. "Dirk, you are a good shopper. I feel fantastic!"

I chuckled. "That's the look I was going for so I can watch you iron your new clothes."

I dressed as she finished ironing and went to put the skirt on. "Not so fast, Doc. First the perfume. A dot behind each ear, one at the base of the throat, one between the boobs, and a last one in your newly groomed pubic hair." She applied the perfume as I had asked, with me watching.

"It's kind of erotic having you watch as I do this."

"That's the idea, and I love it too, Doc."

The room filled with the scent of perfume as she dressed.

I looked her over as put the sandals on, fully dressed. She looked great.

"Erika, you are a vision of loveliness!"

She blushed a little. "Thanks, Dirk. I feel like I am getting ready for the prom!"

I went back to my bag of purchases and pulled out the necklace and earring set. "No outfit would be complete without some jewelry."

She gasped at the open jewelry case. "Oh Dirk, you shouldn't have! Thank you!"

"Turn around and I'll put the necklace on you." I did, then turned her around.

"You look stunning. I'll let you do the earrings. Ah, I see you have not put the lipstick on yet. Good! Now we start the romantic phase of the date." I took her in my arms and kissed her gently on the lips, the very first time we had kissed.

She looked into my eyes for a moment after the kiss, then reached her fingers up and gently stroked my cheek, then returned the same gentle kiss.

She went to the bathroom, put on the new earrings and lipstick, then came out and did a pirouette for inspection and admiration. She was glowing.

I asked, "Again, you look great! Are you starting to feel sexy?"

"I do! I feel like a new woman!"

"In that case, we shall now depart for drinks and dinner."

Walking to the elevator, I took her hand. She looked over at me, surprised.

"It's part of the date package."

She smiled. "I like the date package."

Date Night

In the elevator on the way down, I started doing some thinking. "When are you leaving town, I forgot to ask?"

"Let's see, this is Thursday, right? I fly back Saturday midday. I had Friday planned off to either visit Gina again or do some sightseeing. When do you go back to work?"

"On Saturday late afternoon. I fly to Rome, coming back Monday."

She looked thoughtful. "Hmmm, okay."

I had asked the hotel concierge about a place that would be a good date place for drinks, snacks, and dancing. I followed the directions and after about 10 minutes we pulled in. I held her hand again as we walked in, and the hostess smiled at our cuteness as she seated us.

Erika leaned over to me. "Did you see the way that the hostess looked at us? This dating thing is working!"

"Yes, we look like a couple. We're adorable and now every man in the place will be mad at me because his wife/girlfriend is saying, "Why can't you treat me like that?""

She laughed. "Good data points."

"Just remember the transition point between lust and feelings of love. It's dangerous."

She looked pensive. "The easy part would be to not participate in dating behaviors like kissing and holding hands."

"Yes, but it's fun and sexy."

She smiled. "Indeed, it is."

We ordered drinks and they arrived as the DJ started playing some music. We sat and chatted for a while, enjoying each other and the moment.

She asked, "Do you want to stay with me tonight and do things tomorrow? Are you getting tired of me yet?"

"The way you look right now, it would take a tow truck to pull me away from you. I'd love to hang out with you tomorrow."

"Well, in that case, let me propose something. How about a double date with Gina and Matt tomorrow night if they are available? Would that be awkward? We had been trying to get together when she had her family emergency."

I thought for a minute. "I'm game, but what about you? They will take one look at us and know that we have been fucking our brains out."

She laughed. "Maybe that's the point I want to make with them. Dowdy 70-year-old Erika comes to Atlanta, meets a handsome young pilot, has a makeover, and gets laid."

"I think you have the order wrong. Besides, I'm not young."

"Age is relative, and you have me feeling pretty young, my friend."

I leaned over and kissed her. "You feel pretty young to me, too."

The server had come over to see if we were ready to order. She had seen me kiss Erika and smiled at us. We ordered another drink each, and a savory appetizer. Our afternoon chili dog lunch was still with us, and neither of us wanted an entrée. I for sure did not want to be stuffed when we had sex later.

Stimulation

We started our second drink as the appetizer arrived. After a bit, the DJ played something slow, so I asked her to dance.

She tried to stall. "Dirk, I don't dance!"

"Neither do I. Come on."

We walked to the dance floor hand in hand, joined each other, and swayed back and forth together. It was very pleasant and sexy. She was smiling and enjoying the dance. It was time to ramp up the date behavior. I leaned in for another short kiss, this time my tongue darting into her mouth in an exploratory experiment. After a moment, hers answered. I pulled back with a smile as she was looking into my eyes. "More date behavior?" she asked with a smile.

"Yes Ma'am. It's all included in the package."

Her smile widened. "I love the package."

The slow music ended, and the DJ played something faster, so we walked back to the table and worked on our drinks. I asked, "Do you want to call Gina about tomorrow before it gets too late?"

"Good idea, and I'll use the restroom while I'm up."

"You can call her from here if you want."

"No, I'll go to the foyer or outside so I can hear better."

After she left the table, I went to the DJ booth and handed him 20 dollars. "Hey man, when my girl comes back, can you do two slow songs in a row? I'm trying to get laid."

He laughed. "You got it, my brother. That's one fine looking lady you are with!"

I replied, "Thanks! She's a keeper."

Erika returned and reported that we were on with Gina and Matt for dinner on Friday, time and place TBD. "She asked if they could pick me up, and I said you would."

"So, you didn't tell her I was living in your hotel room?"

She laughed. "No, I did not. Do you think they will figure that out?"

"One word. Yes. When they see the makeover, they will know for sure."

The DJ played a slow song. "C'mon, more dancing."

We resumed our slow swaying together, and I kissed her again, a little longer this time. Her tongue responded nicely. I was also making sure our pelvises were in close proximity. She said, "Dirk, people are watching us."

"Then they will get the idea and emulate us as we get hotter for each other."

She snuggled closer. "I'm hot enough to go back to the room now."

I smiled. "Later, my sweet. You need more stimulation."

She shook her head. "If you say so."

That song ended, and the next began, a classic Nat King Cole number. The DJ was earning his keep. I caught his eye and gave him a thumbs up.

She noticed. "What are you doing?"

"I paid off the DJ to keep playing slow songs until you swooned, so I gave him a thumbs up indicating my approval."

She tucked her face into my neck. "You're so crazy. I may swoon any minute. I feel like I'm in a dream."

"Kiss me, dream girl."

She did, our tongues hungrily seeking each other. After a minute, she looked up at me again, with one hand stroking my hair. "I'm having a good time, Dirk. Dating you is fun."

"I'm having a good time, too."

The slow song ended, and we walked back to our table hand in hand. Several people looked at us and smiled. I asked Erika if she wanted another drink, and she said one more for the road. I got a club soda since I was driving. "Shall we split a dessert?"

We agreed on a nice key lime cheesecake, and after it came and we both had our first bite, I decided to increase the stimulus some more. I leaned over and asked her, "Ready for some more stimulation, Doc?" She looked at me as if I was crazy, then nodded her head.

I slid my chair around, so I was 90 degrees to the table, and our legs were parallel, facing opposite directions. I took her hand on the top of the table, and underneath the table, put my other hand on the inside of her bare thigh, just under the skirt. Erika looked around quickly to see if anyone had noticed, which in the dimly lit area nobody could see. To anyone watching, it would look like I was just getting closer for an intimate conversation or another kiss. Her eyes were fixed on mine.

I slid my hand slowly up her thigh until I reached the red panties. Her eyes got wider. I then ran a finger up and down her labia on the outside of the panties. Her eyes closed. Then I moved in. I put my finger under the panties and ran my finger up and down the very moist lips and went inside for a brief second. Her eyes opened, then rolled back in her head. I thought for a moment she had fainted, but then she looked at me directly again. I removed my hand, leaned in, and kissed her deeply while holding her hand.

Smiling at her, I waited for a reaction. She gave me one. "Damn, Dirk! That almost made me have an orgasm right here! That has got to be the most stimulating thing that I have ever experienced. Take me back to the hotel right now, please!"

"Aren't you going to finish your drink?" I asked innocently.

She drained her glass. "Let's pay up and get out of here!"

We managed to walk out with some dignity, me with a waning erection and her with damp panties and a little wobbly after three drinks. We held hands in silence as I navigated to the hotel, and once on the elevator, I pulled her to me and kissed her again. She responded by pushing her hips into me. We were pretty damned fired up. I then remembered at this hotel chain that the back of the elevator was glass, and anyone looking at the elevator could see us. Well, we were putting on a show.

Entering the room, I managed to say calmly, "We should probably hit the restroom before anything else." We did and reconvened in the living room of the suite.

Achieving a Goal

She came to me and put her arms around me, kissing me hard and long. It was very enjoyable as she was a good kisser and there was a lot of heat in the moment. After coming up for air, she gasped, "Shall we go to the bedroom?"

I said, "No, let's start here."

I led us to the sofa, where we had started out not 24 hours before. I put her across my legs on my lap, and after some kissing, started to unbutton her blouse. She responded by tugging my golf shirt out of my slacks and pulling it off over my head. I fondled her boobs over the sexy red bra and ran my hands all over her torso, and with the skirt open to me, I also caressed her thighs all the way up to the panties, this time tickling the top of her slit where I knew her clit was hiding. She was caressing my chest and stroking the back of my neck and my hair.

After a few minutes of that, I started unbuttoning her skirt while she did the same for my slacks. That necessitated getting up so my slacks could be pulled off, then we rejoined with only our underwear on. I admired the sight of her in the sexy, lacy, undergarments and then unfastened her bra, which hooked in the front. Why weren't all bras that easy? Within seconds, I had a bare tit in my hand that I fondled and played with the nipple, which caused Erika to moan and squirm. She had her fist around my rigid cock and was playing with it in a very enjoyable manner. I hoped I did not come in her hand. I was wound up tight.

I then had an idea. I had us stand up and move to a table chair at the dining table. I sat down and put her on my lap facing away from me, with her legs spread a bit outside mine. I now could reach everything I liked to play with and started by playing with her boobs with one hand while reaching into the sexy red panties with my other. I could also spread her legs more by spreading mine. It's very sexy to spread the woman's legs wide as they are being fingered or fucked. She moaned as I ran my fingers up and down her slit, reaching between the labia with the fingertip. Then I wanted to increase her pleasure.

"Erika, reach your arms behind me and join them behind my neck."

She did so, which caused her chest to be pushed out in a sexy way.

"Now arch your back a little."

As she did, a moan escaped her lips. It was an incredibly sexy pose, and I rewarded her cooperation by slipping a finger deep into her sopping wet vaginal vault. A loud moan and gasp escaped her as I worked my finger deep into her hole and curled it, looking for the elusive G spot. As I found it, her moaning and squirming got more intense. I had a boob in one hand, a finger deep in her hole with the other, and was kissing her neck as she threw her head back against my neck. She was shaking with sensation.

She let go of my neck with one hand and reached between her legs for my cock, which had escaped on its own and was protruding between her pussy lips. After pumping it for a minute, she got both hands under her and rose up, pushed her panties to one side, then guided my rock hard dick into her, sat down, and drove my meat deep into her. A loud groan erupted from her, and her hips started rocking back and forth as I played with her clit and drove my hips into her. After a few minutes of intense pleasure, she was moaning nonstop, worked up to a high level of excitement. I stopped her and told her to get off, turn around and face me, then mount back up.

She rose off my slippery, shiny dick, turned around, and after stripping off her wet panties, threw a leg over me and once again guided my cock deep into her cunt as she straddled me. She let out a loud cry as my dick hit the bottom of the vaginal vault. Her hips started a frenzied motion back and forth, as she recalled the pleasure she experienced the night before with her clit grinding against me. I could smell the intoxicating aroma of her new perfume between her tits as I pumped into her as hard as I could while squeezing and biting her nipples. Her mouth found mine and our tongues frantically searched for each other. Even while kissing, her groans and moans were audible. She was going faster and faster, with cries of pleasure becoming louder and longer.

All at once, she threw her head back, and let loose with a heart-rending cry. "Oh Dirk! I'm coming! I'm coming! Oh god, oh god, oh god! AHHHHHHHH! Oooooooh!" Her motion reached a crescendo, then stopped as she collapsed onto me, out of breath and spent. My cock erupted in a torrent of hot cum shooting into her as I cried out in ecstasy. We held each other for a moment, then her hips started to gently move back and forth. I knew what she wanted, so I pushed gently against her to help her tingling pussy.

She grabbed my head and smothered me in kisses. "Oh Dirk, oh Dirk, oh Dirk! I thought I would never have an orgasm again! You're fantastic! What in the world causes this kind of sexual chemistry? It's unreal!"

"At 70 years old having an orgasm is incredible. I'm proud of you!"

She continued to talk enthusiastically for some minutes, high as a kite. All the while my cock was inside her, and I was perfectly comfortable. I stroked her hair, back, and ass as we sat together. After a while, she said, "I suppose we should clean up. Do we shower together or just wipe each other off?"

"I think a wipedown is sufficient for this round."

We went to the bathroom and wiped each other off with warm, wet washcloths, and got into bed naked. Snuggling, she sighed against my neck. I stroked her hair and pulled her close. "How do you feel?"

"I feel like a young girl, except I never came like that before! I'm telling you, that was intense."

"I hope your neighbors weren't trying to sleep."

She laughed. "I hope it is one of those stuffy professors from my convention, and hope he got an erection hearing us going at it!"

That made me laugh. I love satisfied customers.

She then went over how she remembered the evening. "Let's see. How did this result come about? New clothes, new hair, sexy underwear, getting my nails done, perfume, a gift of jewelry, drinks, dancing, kissing and holding hands…"

"Don't forget trimming your pubic hair."

"All right, we'll refer to that as manicuring the vagina area."

"Keeping the necklace on is sexy."

"Oh yes, that adds to the overall stimulation. Let's not forget the public fondling of my vagina, that was exciting! Dirk, you really orchestrated this whole event! You can work wonders! I'll be glad to write a letter of recommendation for you if you need to convince older women of your prowess."

"Well thanks, Doc. I'll just go with verbal recommendations. Word of mouth is the best reference one can get."

She gave me a deep kiss. "To hell with that, I'm not sharing my lover with anyone."

Stretching and yawning, she then said, "You've worn me out, mister. Let's get ready for bed and rest up for the next time."

"Oh, you think there is going to be a next time, do you?"

She grinned at me. "There better be, I'm counting on it!"

We got ready for bed. She wanted to keep the necklace on, which I thought was sweet. Together we fell into a deep, satisfying sleep.

Friday Morning

We both awoke around the same time and decided to save water by showering together after brushing our teeth. The warm water, good smelling soap I had bought the day before, with the sexual ambiance all contributed to me having a raging erection within minutes. I love showering with women. Even with her wearing a shower cap and 25 years difference in our ages, Erika and I had a sexual connection that was phenomenal.

After washing each other with the fragrant soap and kissing while trying to keep her hair dry, we were locked in a slippery embrace that was going to end up with my cock deep in her pussy. There is no better way to start your day than with a woman that wants you to fuck her brains out before breakfast. I recommend it highly.

We toweled off quickly and fell into bed, with Erika only stopping to dab a few places of her damp skin with the really nice perfume we had bought the day before. She was really getting into the sexy ambiance thing. She still had her necklace and earrings on, which was very sexy. We immediately embraced and started caressing each other. I was learning Erika's hot spots and went right to them. After fondling her boobs and kissing the nipples, my finger started up and down her slit, with the finger parting the labia and sampling the textures within. After a few minutes of that with her groaning appreciatively, I knelt between her legs and put my face straight into her pussy.

Ah, I love a freshly washed pussy straight from the shower. The combination of soap, perfume, and raw Grade A cunt all combined to make an intoxicating scent. I admired the view, and my handiwork in trimming that out-of-control bush into a nicely manicured pussy with smoothly shaved edges along the lips. It looked great. I went right to sticking my tongue into the vaginal vault hole and curled the tip of the tongue to tickle the spot where I got the best reaction the night prior. It was still the right spot, as I heard moaning and groans while her hips started to squirm. I ran my tongue up and down the labia, giving the clit some love on the north end and making sure to get into the hole and stimulate the G spot on the southern pass. Her moaning was an indication that I was on the right track.

I moved up to lay alongside her, and after Erika wiped my face of the pussy juice and saliva that had accumulated, I wrapped my arm around her and put her on her back so I could reach the left boob with my left hand, and the right boob with my right hand. It all worked out, and again I thought how lucky I was to have been blessed with long arms for this kind of work. I can also get things off high shelves in grocery stores. I kissed her deeply as I alternated the right hand with working over her pussy, with my finger running up and down the slit, alternating tickling her clit and rubbing the G spot, which I had evidently found as her hip squirming increased and the moaning was getting louder and more frequent. I love hearing and feeling feedback, it tells me I am in the correct spots and doing things she likes. She was busily pumping my cock while I was doing all this, and I was rock hard with all the attention. After several minutes and lots of moaning and squirming from Erika, I could tell it was time to put the dick into action.

I wanted to up the excitement, so to try something new, I asked her to tell me what she wanted.

"Erika, for fun let's tell each other what we want the other to do, using the naughtiest possible language."

"Okay, that sounds like fun. How do we start?"

"I'll start. What do you want me to do with my cock?"

She got into it immediately. "Oh, stick that hard cock in my wet pussy!"

Whoa! I was getting turned on more with just that one phrase! "I'm going to stick my cock in you and make you beg me to fuck you!"

I knelt between her legs and put the purple head of my dick against her labia, pushing in just a little as she guided the head in. "You're going to have to beg me for it now!"

"Oh please, Dirk! Stick that dick into me!"

Now we were getting the idea! I eased my hips forward and pushed in smoothly all the way to the hilt, until I knew our pubic hair was mingling.

"What do you want now?"

"Fuck me, Dirk! Give it to me, all of it!"

Damn, this was some hot and sexy fun! I complied with her request and started a nice rhythmic thrusting, making sure to get as long a stroke as possible, in and out.

I wanted to let her know I liked it. "Oh, Erika! Your pussy is so tight and wet! It makes me want to come!"

"Don't you dare come yet; I want some hard pounding! Give it to me harder!"

I increased the rate and intensity of my thrusting. "Oh, yeah! Your pussy is feeling good!"

She wanted more; we were pretty worked up. "Lift my legs up, Dirk! Give it to me deeper!"

"You got it! I'm going to spread your legs and get all your pussy!"

"Oh yeah! Spread my legs!"

I was going hard and deep. It felt great. The wonderful scent of her perfume emanated from her overheated body. I pushed her legs up higher. "Cross your ankles behind my neck! I'm gonna drill you hard!"

"Yes! Do it hard! Oh, shit! It feels so good!"

It was so hot, I felt I was going to burst. "Push that hot pussy up against me! Push it harder!"

"Oh yes! I'm pushing your hard cock deep into me! Damn! I'm tingling, I'm about to come!"

"I'm right there with you! Keep it up! Push against me! Push that fucking sweet pussy against me!"

"I am! Shit! I'm hot as shit! Pound my pussy! Oh, shit, I'm about to come!"

Then she let loose with a low howl of intense pleasure. "Oooooooohh! Awwww! Damn! I'm coming! Oh, Dirk, I'm coming! Oh god! Oh God! Ahhhhhhhhh!"

I cut loose with a jet of hot cum deep inside her and joined her in exclaiming my pleasure. "Oh damn, Erika! That was great! You have some damned fine pussy!"

We both slowed down, and I lowered her legs to a more normal position. We were breathing hard with exertion, and some sweat had formed on our brows and chests. I pushed deep within her, getting every ounce of cum that I had into her sweet cunt.

"Oh wow, Dirk! You made me come again! You are a freaking miracle worker. Oh shit, that feels good. Push hard into me! My pussy is tingling!"

I kept the pressure on her pussy, it felt so good. "Damn, Erika! You are amazing! Another orgasm. Woo hoo!" I was so happy for her; her libido had reawakened.

We slowly came back to normal, our breathing slowed, and we tenderly caressed each other and kissed slowly and deeply. I was still inside her, keeping my weight off her by propping myself up on my arms. I heard her sigh deeply.

"Dirk, oh Dirk. This is fabulous. Stay inside me and we'll nap just like this."

"Okay, that sounds fine. I'll roll us over a little so I don't crush you."

We dozed for a while, blissfully unaware of anything but being in physical contact and joined together. After a nice sleepy interval, she roused.

"Let's clean up and head down for breakfast before they close."

"Is food all you think about?"

"No, lately all I think about is having you inside me making me come!"

"I second that thought."

Breakfast with a smile

We wiped each other down and got dressed quickly. This time, on the way to breakfast we kissed while waiting for the elevator, we kissed on the elevator, and we kissed while waiting in line to order. People looked at us and smiled.

"Dirk, people are smiling at us a lot. Do we look like we are in love?"

I grimaced. "This is that threshold between lust and love. We are simulating being in love through our romantic behavior, which is a lot of fun. A very precarious time."

She smiled. "But we are only pretending to be romantic. There is a difference. Tomorrow I am heading back home, and you are going to work. Our lives will continue with wonderful memories of each other."

I looked at her. She looked very happy. Her newly spiked hair looked good, and although she didn't have full makeup on, her eyes were enhanced by a touch of eyeliner. She had the pretty blouse on from last night and her usual cargo pants. It was a look. I knew she had her walking shoes on without looking. The necklace and earring set sparkled. The lines in her face and around her eyes seemed to have softened. She did not look her chronological age but was a mature, confident woman that had been having great sex with a younger man. It was like a tonic. I should find a way to bottle that feeling.

She had noticed me looking at her but did not say anything and smiled. I smiled back.

"Just admiring a pretty lady, don't mind me."

She dimpled. "I believe I know what you are thinking. Freshly... and all that."

"Nothing like it in the world for a breakfast companion."

"What do you want to do today? Besides the obvious. Please keep in mind that I have been running on adrenaline and this old lady needs to rest up a bit before you ravage me again."

I thought for a minute. "Let's get a time and place from Gina on where to meet for dinner, maybe we can plan around that. Do you like civil war history?"

We got coffee to go and went back to the room, managing to only kiss once. Well, maybe twice. She called Gina and coordinated a time and place about halfway between each other's locations. Since we had my truck to get around in, we were very flexible.

Erika got out her laptop. "Dirk, I want to record some notes about our night and all the factors that went into a successful first orgasm and the subsequent one before I forget any details. Do you mind?"

"Not at all. I'll be looking at the local attractions handout for some ideas on where to show you around."

She went into psychologist mode, typing away on her laptop with a small frown of concentration on her face. I admired her again, thinking of how responsive she was to romantic behavior and the makeover. While she had been pretty hot in bed before that, the change was impressive. I wondered if we were getting into trouble by emulating the boyfriend/girlfriend thing. I think I got into trouble with that when Kim and I were together, but that was in a vacation setting. It was fun being romantic and affectionate even knowing it was for a short term. Could we break it off cleanly? Did we want to? Shaking off those thoughts, I looked at the touristy stuff and wrote down some suggestions for when she got done with her note writing.

Erika looked up. "My first successful orgasm last night happened pretty fast, while the first real attempt yesterday was not successful even though there was lots of foreplay. Why do you think that was?"

"I'd say it was all about setting the mood and prolonged expectation. We really started foreplay at the mall yesterday, and it ramped up with everything we did. The romantic date behavior did a lot for setting the stage. Dancing, kissing, sexy underwear, and perfume all played a part. We used a lot of the senses and caused excitement even before we started taking each other's clothes off. In the military, we call it preparing the battlefield."

She smiled. "You did a hell of a good job preparing me for the major event. How about this morning? We did not have to do a lot of the preparation to get me to an orgasm."

"I think that was excitement at the spontaneity and a lot to do with the familiarity of where you liked to be touched, licked, kissed, and so on. You did want to add some perfume before we started and kept your necklace on. All that added up to feeling, looking, and smelling sexy. Besides, you knew you could have an orgasm, so it wasn't hanging over your head with you worrying about it. I think they will happen a lot easier for you from now on."

She reached up and touched her necklace with her fingers and smiled. "I may never take it off. Until I get home, that is. Then I'll put it away until or if I see you again. It's a tradition of sorts. It shall be used for no lesser purpose, etc."

"We'll have to work out if we are going to see each other again."

She looked at me for a moment. "Yes, we will." A moment passed. "Back to research. What do you have in store for me tonight?"

I went to my shopping bag and started pulling things out. "Here we have a mask, blindfold, some clothesline, and this device. I already gave you the Vaseline."

She looked intrigued and picked up the device. "What's this?"

I had to laugh. "It says neck massager but take a look at the shape."

"Oh, my! It's a vibrating dildo!" She laughed.

"No, it's a neck massager, it says so on the packaging. It just happens to vibrate, and the end is shaped like a bullet, for convenient neck massaging. It also just happens to be a convenient shape to allow it to be inserted into various bodily orifices if one so desires. I also have alcohol to sanitize it based on where it was inserted."

She was having a giggling fit now. "Oh, I see. I do hope I can use it for a massage."

"I'll be glad to help you."

She was still smiling. "What's the other stuff for?"

"The clothesline can be used for light bondage, tying you to the bed or whatever. The mask and blindfold are for fantasy play if you want to try it. The Vaseline is if you decide to try anal sex."

"Hell, you have me trying everything else, I might as well try anal sex. I'm already titillated about the fantasy play. How does that work?"

It was my turn to smile. "Think about the possibilities during the day and at dinner with Gina."

"Oh, you're a naughty man! I am getting excited already." She pulled me close and kissed me deeply. "What shall we do between now and dinner?"

"I've got some ideas. Do you like the movie, 'Gone with the Wind?'"

"Yes, it's a classic."

"We could visit the Margaret Mitchell house, where the author lived. There is also a cool civil war diorama called the Cyclorama that's a must-see. Then we could go by Stone Mountain and see some really neat carvings of Civil War Generals on the side of a granite mountain. After all that, it will probably be time to meet Gina and Matt."

"Sounds perfect! I'd like to do all that. What are we wearing?"

I thought for a minute. "The second outfit we got you, the blouse and shorts. You can wear the sandals, there won't be a lot of walking. Do you want to do another application of the tanning stuff? That will look great with the white shorts."

"Whatever you think, Dirk. I am learning to go along with whatever you suggest."

"Good, I have plans for you." I went back to the shopping bag and handed her another bra and panty set, this time in black. Erika exclaimed.

"Dirk! You are such a planner! Do you want me to put these on now?"

"Only if I get to help you with the bra. I want to watch you iron your outfit and my slacks wearing just that."

She had a big smile. "Preparing the battlefield again?"

"Yes, Ma'am!"

I helped her into the bra and panties, taking great care to help with the breasts. The iron and board were still out from the day before, so I enjoyed watching her iron for us in the sexy underwear. I got dressed, and when she started to put the clothes on, I stopped her.

"I want to watch you put the perfume on."

She smiled at that and made a show of putting the little dabs in all the right places, grinning as she put some down in her panties. "That's for you."

"Much appreciated!"

Once dressed, she did a turnaround in front of me like a fashion model.

I smiled at her. "Very nice! Too bad I'll be taking all that off you later."

She laughed. "Better be sure to wait until we get back to the hotel before you do that!"

We left the hotel and toured Atlanta, visiting the sights we had discussed and ending up at the restaurant to meet Gina and Matt right on time. Erika had asked me several times about the fantasy play, and I just smiled at her.

Double Date

We got out of the truck and were about to enter the restaurant, when I asked Erika, "How do you want to handle this? Holding hands as boyfriend and girlfriend or play it cool and pretending we are just friends?"

She pondered that for a moment. "Let's hold hands like we have been doing all day, and not say anything else. I'm sure they will catch on. I think kissing in front of them may be a bit much."

"Got it."

We entered and found them waiting in the foyer for a table. They both exclaimed over Erika's appearance.

Gina asked, "What made you decide to try a new look?"

Erika smiled at me. "Dirk suggested a makeover to help me achieve a goal."

Well, that was mysterious enough. Gina looked at me. I could tell she wanted more but was too polite to ask.

After small talk, we were seated and placed our drink orders. Gina was about to burst. "Well, what have you guys been up to?"

Erika fielded the question. "Oh, Dirk has been showing me some things. We've spent some nice quality time together."

Gina wanted more. "Where have you visited? Anything interesting?"

Erika listed the places we saw today, implying that the sightseeing was over a series of days rather than all in one day. They seemed satisfied.

Matt chimed in. "Sounds like Dirk has kept you busy, Erika."

Erika laughed, "Yes, he has kept me moving."

We ordered dinner, Erika and I sharing an entrée like I usually do. I am really trying to watch my weight as I get older, and eating a full meal when out makes it tough. We managed to keep our hands off each other, but it was hard.

After the meal, the conversation between Gina and I evolved to work things, which we tried to cut short. She mentioned that the bids would be out tomorrow, and we would have our schedules for next month. That quieted me down for a few minutes, as I knew that I would need to spend some time with Kim and get our relationship sorted out. I also needed to respond to Tina and work that situation out. All this while fucking Erika. Maybe I should enter a monastery.

There were no disasters that pulled Gina away tonight, and we had a nice time visiting. Erika and Gina reminisced about the time they were neighbors and had several funny stories about their neighborhood and the folks that lived there. We parted ways and headed for our respective vehicles to join the Atlanta Friday night traffic.

As we got underway, I commented, "That was nice. I'm glad you suggested having dinner with them."

Erika looked at me, "I hope it wasn't awkward for you. I think Gina wanted to ask a lot more about what we really have been doing."

"I think you're right. I'm sure we are the main topic of conversation on their ride home."

She reached across the truck and put her hand on my thigh. "My main topic centers around what we are going to do once at the hotel. It was hard to keep my hands off you at dinner."

I laughed. "Doctor Erika! Are you exhibiting signs of wanton lust towards a younger man?"

"Yes, I am! And I must say I am relishing the feeling. Can you come home with me to keep satisfying my sexual urges?"

"I think the company would take a dim view of me being away. Sorry."

She looked at me again, her hand squeezing my thigh. "What are we going to do, Dirk? Continue to see each other or call this romantic interlude over when I get on the plane tomorrow?"

I thought for a minute. "Both scenarios have benefits and drawbacks. I really enjoy being your friend and very much enjoy being your lover. Will you use your newly discovered sexual appetite when you get back home, or are you going to wait for me to make a sexual service call?"

"Do you mean am I going to have sex with men back home?"

"Yes, are there any likely candidates?"

She let go of my thigh and looked out the window. "There are a few men that are hinting around about going on a date. I wonder what their reaction would be when they see my red underwear as I was asking them to perform oral sex?"

I laughed. "I hope you screen them for cardiovascular health before that. You may be calling 911 in your panties."

She laughed as well. "Now, there is an image!"

Then she got serious. "I suppose I will try sex with some men back home, but like you, I don't want a long-term relationship. Do you have any girlfriends that you have ruined for life and only want sex with you?"

"Yes, there are a few that want me to be their only sex partner, but I encourage all my friends to enjoy sex with other men. I'd be proud and pleased if you would call me in a month and told me you had a great experience."

She put her hand back on my thigh. "You are an unusually secure and unselfish man, Mister Dirk."

"Thank you. Here we are back at our love nest."

Fantasy Island

We walked through the lobby holding hands, and once in the elevator shared a kiss. Entering the room, she looked at the paraphernalia on the table and then looked at me.

"Well, Dirk. Do you want to watch TV or start ravishing me with these implements?"

I tried to look innocent. "Are there any good movies you'd like to see?"

She punched me in the shoulder. "Jerk! You had better get ready to show me what all this is for! I need more data points. And some more sex in case you haven't noticed. This is our last night together and I need to finish up my exploration of all things Dirk."

I rubbed my shoulder. "You are exhibiting signs of aggression. Are you sexually repressed?"

She laughed and came over to put her arms around me and kiss me deeply. "I am anything but repressed with you, my dear friend and sex mentor. You know how to show a girl a good time. Now quit teasing me and tell me what we are doing next."

"How about some light bondage, then fantasy role playing, then anal sex if you still want to. During the bondage, I'll try the vibrator on you."

"Wow! That sounds like a lot. I suppose I'm all in on this research thing. Let's do it!"

I loved her enthusiasm. "Let's hit the restroom and meet in the bedroom."

Collecting the clothesline, scissors, mask, blindfold, vibrator and Vaseline, I made a pile of the stuff at the foot of the bed. She joined me, with fresh lipstick and her makeup tweaked. She looked excited.

"Strip for me, then I'll arrange your naked body on the bed, then tie you up."

She looked even more excited. Stripping down slowly and carefully hanging her outfit up, she seductively slid her bra and panties off and stood naked in front of me. After letting me admire her for a moment, she crawled onto the bed and lay there, awaiting instructions.

I ran the clothesline around the headboard and carefully tied one of her wrists. Then I pulled the clothesline around and with her arms spread wide above her head, tied the other wrist, and cut off the remaining rope. I then tied the end of the line to one ankle, and gently pulled it to the corner of the bed, securing the rope to the bedframe. I did the same with the other ankle and stepped back to admire my handiwork. Her arms and legs were bound, with her spread eagled on the bed. She could move a little but was now my captive.

"Erika, this is very important. If you want me to stop what I'm doing, say the words, 'GO, GO, GO' so I'll know to stop or let you go. Sometimes the word 'Stop' comes out involuntarily. So that's our safe word. I'll immediately stop what we are doing and cut you loose. Let's practice. Say the words to get me to stop what I'm doing."

She dutifully recited, "GO, GO, GO."

"Perfect. How are you feeling?"

"Excited, sexy, and nervous. I'm totally under your control! It's a little unnerving."

"Great! Ready for some role-playing? Do you want to be a little scared during this? I absolutely promise not to hurt you."

She looked even more excited. "I think a little scary would be exciting."

"Okay, here is the scenario, but I am holding back some details to provide some excitement. I put the blindfold and gag on you. Then I leave the room and come back in as a stranger who has his way with you. How's that?"

She squirmed with excitement. "I think you are leaving out some details."

"Of course, I am. Ready?"

She took a deep breath. "Ready!"

I put the blindfold on, covering her eyes, and wrapped a scarf around her neck, through her mouth. She had a very light gag on, that if she needed to, she could call out the safe words.

"Erika, you are ready."

She nodded vigorously.

I left the room and looked at my watch. I waited exactly one minute, it would seem a lot longer to someone tied up naked spreadeagled on a hotel bed.

Back in the bedroom, I stood at the bedside with her wallet I had gotten out of her purse/backpack. "Erika? I'm sorry to have to do this to you, but I need the money. I have your wallet."

I lifted her blindfold a moment so she could see. Her face showed her puzzlement.

I continued. "I'm very sorry, but I have to do this. I made an arrangement with one of the maintenance guys that has been watching us. He approached me and wants to fuck you. He's giving me $500. I really need the money. While he's here fucking you, I'm going down to the ATM machine and get cash out your checking account. I found your PIN number while you were sleeping. You should really be more careful."

Her face looked confused and a little frightened. I left the room, made a noise like I was picking up the room phone out in the living room, and said loudly enough so she could hear, "Yeah, it's me. She's ready for you. All tied up like you wanted. Bring the cash." Then I hung up. I waited another two minutes and knocked on the door from the inside. I opened and closed the door and pretended to have a conversation with someone. Then I opened and closed the door and went into the bedroom.

There, I sat on the side of the bed. She called out through the gag, "Dirk? Is that you?"

I whispered harshly, "Your boyfriend is not here, princess. I've got you all to myself."

She squirmed and her face showed anxiety.

Whispering again, I said, "He did a real good job tying you up. I'm gonna have some fun with you now. You just lay back and enjoy."

I then put on some surgical gloves I had bought at the variety store and started roughly fondling her boobs. She jumped in surprise and struggled against the ropes. I ran my hands down her body, knowing that the feel was very different than a ungloved hand. I ran my hand down her pussy and pushed a gloved finger into her.

"Now, that's some fine pussy, right there. Your boyfriend told me it was real nice. Now I'm gonna find out." I started finger fucking her, and she squirmed in fear or excitement, it was hard to tell.

"Oh yeah, that's some fine pussy. Now I'm gonna fuck you!"

I pulled a condom onto my hard dick and crouched between her legs as she struggled to get away.

"Now, princess, don't you even try and get away. I'm gonna have a good old time with your pussy."

I slipped my cock into her and gave a few hard thrusts. She was struggling and making sounds behind the gag. None of them was the safe word. I lay on her and humped away. After a bit, I grunted and groaned like I had come, then pulled out and climbed off the bed.

"You did real good, princess. Just keep your mouth shut about this and you won't get hurt."

I left the room, and opened and closed the door, making some stray conversational sounds. After a minute by the watch, I went to her. She was laying motionless.

"Hey, Erika. It's over. I'm going to take off your blindfold now."

I gently pulled her blindfold off, and her gag. She blinked as she looked up at me.

"Damn, Dirk! That was some serious fantasy play. For a while, I was getting frightened! How did you come up with that?"

I smiled, "I've got a good imagination. Want me to untie you now?"

"Yes! Then hold me! I'm still a little frightened."

I untied her, then gave her a big hug. "What did you think?"

She shook her head. "I can see where some women would get off on that. I felt strong sexual urges, fear of rape, and elation when it was over. It felt so different, is that why the gloves? Even your dick felt different. Did you come?"

"That's why I used gloves and a condom so you would experience a different feel. No, I didn't come, I simulated it. Did it feel real?"

"Yes! Wow, what an experience." She shivered.

"Are you cold?"

"Just still a little shaken up. Get into bed with me and let's snuggle until I calm down."

I stripped down and got into bed, pulling the covers over us and holding Erika close, stroking her hair as we lay together.

I felt responsible. "I'm sorry if that was too intense."

"It's okay, Dirk. I feel better now that we are snuggling. What's next?"

Vibrating is Stimulating

"Your next experience will be a lot more fun. I'll tie you up again, then try out the vibrator on your lady parts until you scream with delight."

She smiled as she wiggled closer to me. "That does sound like fun. Will this involve you putting your dick in me? Since you didn't get to come during the rape scenario, I owe you one."

"That can be arranged, and I must say I like the way you think. Is that your hand stroking my cock? It's quite pleasant."

"Who, me? Quiet, nerdy, meek, dowdy, elderly college professor and psychologist rubbing a younger man's dick in a hotel room in a strange city? It certainly doesn't sound like me."

"Somehow elderly does not fit you any more than any of those other descriptive terms. Turn a little so I can play with your boobs, Mmmmm. That's better. I better tie you up again before I get sidetracked."

"Let me go to the restroom first."

I tied her up again, this time leaving the blindfold off. I got out the vibrator and tried it against my cheek to see what it felt like, then started working her over with it, first around her nipples, then each boob, then straight down to the pussy.

I applied the vibrator to the skin around the clit, gently at first and then a little more firmly. She squirmed and bucked her hips. I asked, "Are you trying to get away from it?"

She grinned. "It's a weird sensation, kind of a combination of irritating and stimulation. Where else are you going to use it?"

"Wait and see, Doc. Wait and see."

I parted her labia with two fingers and slid the vibrator into the gap, then started moving it up and down her slit. Her reaction was immediate.

"Oh, wow. Oh, boy. Oh, my that's intense. Don't stop!"

I then put the snout of the device into the hole of her vaginal vault. She liked that, too.

"Ahh, oh boy. Oh, boy. Ahhhhhh!"

After a few minutes of intense stimulation, I looked up at her face, strained in concentration with her lower lip between her teeth. "Feel good?"

She looked at me like I was an idiot. "Hell, yes! It feels wild. Damn!"

I then moved the thing up to her clit while I put my finger deep within her and tickled her G spot. Her hips bucked and convulsed as a steady stream of moaning came out of her mouth. After a minute of this, I reached up squeezed her nipples and resumed a more direct attack on the clit.

"Oh, Dirk! I'm going to come! Ahhhhhhhh! Ohhhhhh. Oh, God! Oh, God! Oh, hell! Ahhhhhhh!"

While she had her hips bucked up off the bed I quickly moved the vibrator and applied it to her asshole. I thought she was going to break the ropes.

"Oh, good god! What the hell? Aw, no! Ahhhhhhhh!"

I removed the stimulus as she came back to earth, sweating and gasping for breath. I gently stroked her boobs and her clit. She became aware of me again.

"Get on me, Dirk! Get that cock in me while I am still tingling!"

I was happy to comply. My iron hard dick must have thought I had forgotten about him, and he gladly entered the slippery wet pussy and went to work. I was so turned on by her being turned on, I thrust away in hard, long strokes as she wiggled and bucked under me.

She gasped, "Dirk! Untie my legs so I can wrap them around you!"

I did, and she did, pulling me in deeper as her hips bucked into me wildly. I was thinking she was done with her orgasm when she started heavy groaning and moaning again.

"Oh, Dirk! Fuck me hard! Harder! Lift my legs up!"

I got the message, and complied, ending up with her feet at my eye level.

"Harder! Harder!"

Wow, she was still in the game. More moaning came out, getting louder by the minute. I squeezed her nipples and fondled her tits. She said, "Kiss me!"

While kissing her, playing with her nipples, and thrusting madly into her with her legs in the air, I began to realize she was about to come for the second time. While kissing, a deep growl of pleasure came out of her throat, then she threw her head back and uttered a loud cry of pure pleasure.

"Oooooohhhh God! Oh, God! Ahhhhhhh! Damn! Ahhhhhhhh! I'm coming again!"

I kept up the thrusting while the waves of orgasm swept over her, with my cock erupting in spasms of hot cum blasting deep within her as I cried out. Then she went limp suddenly, so I lowered her legs and stopped my attack on her sopping wet pussy. She moaned softly and rolled back and forth against the ropes, her legs still around me and my cock within her.

"Oh, Dirk! What the hell has gotten into me? This is fantastic!"

I stroked her hair and kissed her gently. "Want me to untie you now?"

"No, I want to stay like this forever. Don't move. Just stay in me. Ah, this is so good."

"If the faculty could only see you now!"

She laughed so hard my cock got pushed out. "Yes, I would be the envy of the staff. Whew! What is it about you?"

I untied her, and we collapsed into each other's arms.

I stroked her cheek and told her, "You know, you're pretty damned sexy for a 70-year-old. I am proud of you! Two orgasms in one session? Amazing!"

She smiled at me. "When you put that vibrator against my anus, I thought my body was on fire!" She thought for a minute. "I'm taking that damned thing home with me!"

"You got it, Doc. Just don't pack it in your carry-on baggage. TSA will see it in the x-ray machine, then pull it out and play with it in front of everyone."

That got a laugh out of her. "Good advice!"

We got our breathing back under control, and I looked at her wrists for any red marks from the ropes. There was a little irritation, but it would not lead to bruising. I hoped, anyway.

"Let's get cleaned up and take a nap."

We wiped down and then got back into the bed.

"Remind me to pick up the ropes and take them with me, I don't want the housekeeping staff wondering what was going on in here!"

She laughed again. "It would only enhance my reputation."

Trying the Back Door

We dozed off while spooning and slept for a couple of hours before she got up to use the restroom. Climbing back in bed, she could tell I was awake. "I woke up remembering something about trying anal sex?"

I looked at her in disbelief. "Doc, it's up to you. I'm game if you are. Besides, it's the middle of the night."

"I want to try it. Lord knows I've tried everything else so far! Then I think it's back to plain old boring straight missionary fornication."

"Fornication with you has never been boring, my Dear."

"Thanks. How does this work? Same foreplay and stimulation and then you just put it in my anus?"

"Pretty much. We'll give your pussy some love first and then I'll slip it up your ass, properly lubricated for maximum comfort, of course."

"Of course. You may begin stimulation. Start with kissing my boobs, then me, then finger my pussy."

I laughed. "You got it. Please try to not be so shy about what you want this time."

"I'll try to be more involved in the process. Ah, that's nice. Good work so far!"

As I was kissing her boobs, I caught a faint smell of the perfume I had watched her apply what was now yesterday. It was heavenly. I played with her boobs and nipples as I ran a finger up and down her labia, poking into the vaginal vault every now and then, gently as I knew a lot of activity had taken place there, and I knew it would be tender. After a few minutes of this very pleasant activity, her hips woke up and she began squirming against me.

"Put it in me, please."

I placed the head of my once again rock hard cock against her lips and pushed in gently, with her sighing in bliss as it made its way to the bottom of her vagina.

"Just fuck me slowly for a couple of minutes, then you can put it in my ass."

Her language during sex was not what I would have thought when I first met her. It turned me on, not that I needed much help. She and I had a very strong sexual chemistry, something I would have never thought the first time we met, just a few days ago. She had felt it, and I was glad she was forthright about wanting to see what it was all about.

I gave her a nice, smooth and satisfying stroking, in and out for a few minutes. Then she said, "Let's do it."

I had her roll over in the doggie style position and took the tin of Vaseline from the bedside table and applied a gob of it on her anus, then gently worked it in with my finger. She moaned a little as my finger entered her asshole. I then greased up my cock, and with another gob of the jelly on the purple knob of my dick, placed it against her asshole. She braced herself on hands and knees, totally giving herself to me.

I asked, "Ready?"

"Yes. Is it going to hurt?"

"It may hurt a little as the tissue gets stretched out, then it will be pressure and some intense feeling. Let me know if you want me to stop or pull out. Just say stop or pull out."

"Okay. I trust you. That's the way your finger felt. I can feel you pushing on the anus. You can push it in now, slowly, please."

"Yes, Ma'am!" She giggled. Man, she was one adventurous senior citizen.

I pushed against the initial resistance of the anus until my glans got on the other side of the sphincter, then waited for a reaction.

She had one. "Ohh, that is some sensation. Can you wait a minute?"

'Yeah, I'm going to go a little bit at a time, then wait until you tell me to stop or I'll keep going until I'm all the way in."

After a minute, she said, "It's better now. You were right about the stretching. Wow, that is intense."

"Okay, here is some more." I eased in another inch or two and waited again.

She said, "Oh. That's a lot. Stay there a minute. I can't believe I am having you do this to me."

I waited and caressed her ass and boobs for something to do.

"A little more. Wow. That's some kind of feeling."

I pushed in a little more. "I can start in and out a little, so you can see what that's like."

"Yeah, go ahead."

I started a gentle back and forth pumping.

She had an opinion. "That's not too bad but be careful going deeper."

"Okay, let me know when to go deeper."

After a few minutes of gentle pumping, she was ready for more.

"You can go deeper, it's feeling better."

"Here we go." I pushed in a little more and waited for feedback.

"That's not too bad. Keep going. Rub my nipples a little, please."

I complied and gave her clit a little tickle for good measure. I pushed in a little more, being careful not to overwhelm her. A few minutes later of slow progress, I announced, "I'm all the way in."

She was shocked. "So, your cock is all the way up my ass?" She really was into the bedroom dirty talk, I loved it. She took a moment to visualize the length of my shaft up inside her. "Okay, fuck me real slow."

I started a gentle in and out thrusting, enjoying the squeeze of her around my swollen dick. I checked on how she was doing. "How's that feeling?"

"It's an intense kind of pressure, but tolerable. Do a lot of women like this?"

I had to chuckle. "For a few women I know, that's all they want to do. I can reach around and get a finger in the pussy, but it's difficult sometimes."

"Mmmm. Rub my clit and boobs some more."

I did, to the accompaniment of some good moaning. She was not going to come but was not screaming for me to stop either. "How you doing, Doc?"

"I'm content with what is happening. The clit rubbing and boob fondling is quite pleasurable. The ass fucking is very different, I must say. Are you going to come?"

"I'd say very soon. This is really tight. There is a lot of great sensation."

She turned me loose. "You can go faster if you need to come, I'm good."

I pumped a little faster, and in a few minutes felt my balls load up for another salvo. I gasped, "I'm about to come!"

She pushed her ass back into me and wiggled it back and forth for added enjoyment. This was heavenly! I took a moment to appreciate the situation. It was 3 in the morning, and I was fucking a 70-year-old college professor and psychologist in the ass after a couple of nights of exploratory sex. What an experience!

My balls said it was time to go and sent a load of cum through my throbbing cock deep into Erika's ass. After a few spasms, I collapsed onto her, and she wiggled her ass back into me again. That was a really nice move. I stayed in her for the moment as I caught my breath.

"You can stay in me for a minute if you want to, Dirk."

I was still out of breath from the exertion. "Thanks!"

I caressed her boobs, back, and ass while I was enjoying the moment, and was surprised when she reached back and cupped my balls with her hand. "That feels nice!"

She giggled, a very nice thing to do with my rapidly shrinking shaft up her ass. "I heard about that from one of my patients. I recall at the time it sounded interesting. How did it feel?"

"It felt great, thanks!"

I pulled back slowly, my dick coming out of her ass with a wet plop sound. I reached for some tissue to wipe her ass with. I took a moment to enjoy the sight of my cum leaking out of her asshole. It's the little things in life that make you smile.

We rolled off the bed with the tissue crammed between her butt cheeks to keep the leakage under control, and she went straight to the toilet to drain what she could from her asshole. It was one of those moments I had no idea what to say.

She joined me back in the bed with a tee shirt on, ready to sleep. "Oh, Dirk. That was another of many intense experiences I have had with you. Thanks for being my sex coach and mentor."

"I'm glad to be a participant in this research project. What time do you have to get up for your flight?"

"It's not until early afternoon, so if I get there by noon I should be okay. We can set a clock for 9am and be fine."

"My show time is not until 5pm, I can take you to the airport."

She smiled. "That would be lovely."

I had to ask. "How is your bottom? Any pain?"

She looked thoughtful. "Some discomfort, but not as bad as I thought it would be. I almost asked you to give me a good pounding, now I am glad I didn't."

"How about some sleep? You have worn me out."

She smiled again. "I hope you have a little energy left for the morning."

"Doctor Erika! You are insatiable!"

She grinned. "Said the man that made me that way." She gave me a sweet kiss. "Goodnight, Dirk."

"Goodnight, Erika."

Saturday Morning

We both awoke before the alarm went off and after the usual morning routines, ended up in the shower again. Imagine that. We both enjoyed a warm, soapy, fragrant interlude with lots of kissing and embracing while making sure each other's parts were nice and clean. She wore the shower cap to keep her spiky hair dry, and still had the necklace on. It was a sexy combination of different items, much appreciated by me. My cock appreciated it, too and was standing at attention once again. With a smile, her soapy fist closed around it and gave it a gentle stroking, which felt fabulous. Without a word, she turned the water off and once again we hurriedly toweled off and headed for the bed. She had stopped to put a few dabs of perfume on various strategic parts. Preparing the battlefield. Very important.

The last several times I had parted ways with different girlfriends, they had wanted the last session to be lovemaking rather than frantic sex. This time, I was ahead of the game.

"Erika? Let's make love slowly and gently this time, since it's our last."

She smiled. "Dirk, you took the words right out of my mouth. What a sweet idea. You really are a considerate man."

I tried to look modest. "I try."

We lay together on our sides, facing each other. Kissing seemed to be the thing to do, so I started a round of that while gently fondling her boobs. As her skin warmed while she became aroused, the scent of perfume wafted up where we could smell it.

"Great idea on the perfume."

She smiled as she reached for my cock. "I thought you would like it. Not that you need any help getting hard. To think before our first time, I worried that you might not be able to get an erection with an old saggy lady like me."

"I'm telling you; we have a fantastic sexual chemistry."

"I'd heard of something similar in clinical studies. Women were asked why they had sex with a man they did not know or had a romantic relationship with. The answer was, I had to. In our case, the attraction was almost overwhelming. I felt it as soon as we met."

My hand had made it down to her pussy, where I entertained myself by stroking the labia gently while we talked. I could feel the combination of damp pubic hair and pussy juice from her getting aroused. Sticking just the tip of my finger between the lips while running it up and down the slit, I started kissing her boobs all over, lifting them up where they sagged and kissing underneath where the skin was quite warm. Then I kissed her between the boobs and drew in the scent of that lovely perfume. Kissing of the nipples was in order, so I got on with that pleasant task. She was moaning softly, and her hips squirmed as she became hotter.

After a few minutes of that, she asked, "Dirk? Can you please give me some oral for just a minute, then get on me?"

"Of course, Madam. Your wish is my command!" That got a giggle out of her.

I crouched between her knees and gently spread her legs wide open, much wider than needed to make this as sexy as possible. I put my face close to her crotch and admired the labia, the clit, and the neatly trimmed pubic hair. I really did a nice job of trimming. I bent down and took in the symphony of scents, the soap, the perfume, and the sweet smell of wet cunt. I love eating freshly washed pussy. With my fingers I spread the lips and put the tip of my tongue directly into her hole, not touching the sides. I could hear a sharp intake of her breath as she experienced the feeling of my eager tongue entering her.

A loud moan came from above me. "Oh, that's nice! Stick your tongue way in!"

I knew what she was after, so I put the tongue way in and curled the tip up to try and catch the G spot. I must have hit it, as her hips moved up into me and more moaning ensued.

"That's it, Dirk. That's it!"

I gave her favorite spot direct attention for a minute or two, driving her wild as her hips thrashed and she moaned nonstop. She finally gasped, "That's good! Get on me!"

I sat up and rolled on my side. She wiped my face with a cloth that was on standby, then surprised me by pushing me on my back. She said breathlessly, "I almost forgot. Your turn!" and proceeded to take my cock in her mouth and start an enthusiastic blow job.

As she bobbed her head up and down on my iron hard cock, she ran her tongue around the shaft and circled the glans as I had taught her. It felt great, and I told her so. Then she raised her head with some saliva dripping from her chin and said, "Finger me while I'm doing this!"

That's a benefit of having long arms. I was able to reach her pussy and get my finger in while she resumed sucking my dick. After a couple of minutes, she rose up and lay on her back. "Stick that cock in me!"

I gladly complied and started what I hoped was a gentle, sweet motion. She was pretty wound up, and pushed her hips up into me, meeting every thrust. I had to ask. "What happened to slow and sweet lovemaking?"

She grinned at me. "We always seem to go with our strengths, which is fucking hard! We'll talk romantically on the way to the airport. Now fuck me!"

I was also pretty worked up, so I started a hard thrusting, which I could tell she enjoyed by her hip motion and loud groaning. I was enjoying the riding time and was trying hard not to come too quickly when she had a request.

"Dirk, take me to the chair where I had my first orgasm. I want to straddle you in the chair!"

That sounded like a wonderful idea. I pulled out and we got up and staggered out to the living room. I sat down, and she mounted me like she had been doing it her entire adult life. She eased her wet pussy down the shaft of my slimy cock until she was all the way down. A loud groan came from her mouth.

"Damn, did your cock get bigger? It's in so deep!" That was a nice ego boost, but it did not grow magically during the session. Well, maybe it did.

She started grinding her hips back and forth on my pelvis pushing the clit against me, as I tried to shove my dick through her with hard thrusts. I found a boob that needed attention and fondled that and played with the nipple while kissing her deeply. We were both about to explode. After a few short minutes of this activity, her moaning reached a crescendo and she announced what was happening.

"Oh! Oh! Oh! I'm coming! Oh, God! I'm coming! Ahhhhhhhh! Oh, Dirk!"

With that, I came hard and shot a salvo of cum deep into her as her pussy pulsated and the orgasm swept through her. We slowed our frantic movement to a more sedate rhythm and kissed again. After a minute, she stopped and put her arms around me and buried her face into my neck while she kissed it.

"That was as good as the first time. I really wanted to recreate that moment, it felt so damned good!"

"I'll work harder at getting you excited next time."

She laughed, and gave me a playful wiggle of her hips, as my cock was still inside her, which felt great. She looked down at us. We had cum, saliva, sweat, and pussy juice all over us and were still breathing hard. "I'd say we wasted that shower."

"No shower with you is wasted," I said gallantly.

She climbed off and we decided to just wipe each other down. She said, "I want some of you on me and in me as I fly home. Is that corny?"

I smile. "No, it's kind of romantic."

"Also, a little sticky." She took my wrist and looked at my watch, then sighed. "I suppose we should get dressed and check out. After breakfast, of course."

I laughed. "All you think about is sex and eating!"

"They are both appetites, Dirk. One is physical and the other emotional."

I went to the shopping bag that was still on the table. "Here, I have a final gift for you to wear." I pulled out another sexy bra and panty set, this time in white lace.

She was astounded. "Oh, Dirk! How thoughtful. I can feel sexy on my ride home. You must have bought out the store! Come here, you wonderful man!" She hugged me tightly and kissed me hard.

She released me and said, "I get the bathroom first to make myself look good for you."

She went about doing the things that women do to get ready, and I assessed my shirts and found the least wrinkled one she had hung in the closet. The slacks were okay, so I put those on along with the last pair of new underwear I had bought. Once I shaved, I would be presentable. I found the vibrator in the bedroom and put it in her suitcase that she would check as luggage after taking the batteries out. No sense in creating a security scare if the thing came on somehow.

After a bit, she came out with freshly combed hair, makeup on, with fresh lipstick, wearing the last of the new outfits we had bought. This was a nice flowery print blouse that she put on over the navy skirt. The necklace and earrings showed up nicely. I could tell she had put on a little more perfume. She looked fantastic, and I told her so.

"Thank you, sir! I feel like a new woman, confident, stylish, and sexy. It's a great feeling!"

"Your male students will be lusting after you instead of listening to you lecture."

She laughed. "Nobody listens anyway."

We packed up her suitcase, looking around for anything left behind, and she packed up her laptop in the backpack. My luggage was a shopping bag and a laundry bag, both stuffed with dirty clothes.

I said, "The backpack does not go with your outfit. You need one of those clutch purse things."

She laughed. "I'll tell everyone the backpack is yours. Let's go, I'm starving!"

Over breakfast, she brought up a subject we had been avoiding. "Where do we go from here, Dirk? Neither of us wants a long-term relationship. Should we make plans to see each other occasionally? Or break it off altogether?"

I thought for a minute. "I don't think we can recreate the magic of these past few days, which has been incredible. I like you very much as a friend and enjoy our sexual chemistry. You are so easy to talk to, I'd like to stay in touch. Should we meet for sex? I think we should play that by ear. If you feel the urge, call me and we'll talk about it. To be truthful, that may depend on what I work out with Kim."

She looked at me. "And Tina."

"Oh, crap. You're right."

She took my hand across the table. "Dirk, this is the most serious conversation we have had to date. You need to know that you will always be my dear friend and that we have had some wonderful times together, mostly in bed which shades our feelings. If I call you and want to meet, it's probably for sex and companionship. You should not attach any romantic meaning to that. You need to work out with Kim and to a lesser extent Tina what the next steps are."

I sipped my coffee and pondered what she had said. "I'm just not sure if I am ready for a relationship with Kim that could be construed by her as falling in love."

She looked at me. "Aren't you a little bit in love with Kim?"

"I think so, but firmly believe that it's a result of a lot of sex and boyfriend/girlfriend romantic activity causing a false positive on the love test."

"Well, then have a fun summer screwing your brains out with her and reassess the relationship in the fall."

"What about Tina?"

"Let me see if you already know the answer. Suppose you and Kim are being exclusive boyfriend/girlfriend over the summer. What would Kim's reaction be if you asked her if she minded you seeing Tina for sex?"

"I see your point."

She smiled. "Sometimes you already know the answer and just have to say it out loud. Keep Tina at arm's length for the summer until you decide what to do about Kim. And keep me away, I will want to have sex with you if I see you, and don't want to interfere with you and Kim."

I sighed. "This is all so complicated. Okay, you and I will stay in touch and not meet for sex unless the thing with Kim does not work out. She may not even want to get back together."

Still smiling, she said, "All you have to do is ask her."

"You're right, Doc. I need to do that sooner than later. What if you get horny, can you tap into the manpower pool back home?"

She giggled. "I'll have you to think about on cold and lonely nights."

"Don't forget I'm sending the vibrator home with you."

Erika laughed so hard I thought coffee would come out of her nose. She finally gasped, "That's right! I have a new battery powered man substitute! Oh, my that was funny."

I looked at my watch. "I'd better get you on the road, the TSA in Atlanta can take forever to get through."

Goodbye to Erika

We checked Erika out, loaded her luggage and my laundry bags into the truck, and headed to the airport. I decided to park in the short-term lot near the terminal and walk her to her gate.

She objected. "You don't have to do that, Dirk. I can do it on my own."

"It's the least I can do for you. Nobody should have to transit the Atlanta airport on their own. Besides, we can talk more while you are waiting."

She smiled. "In that case, I accept your offer."

We got her boarding pass, and navigated through security, me using my aircrew ID badge to get through. Atlanta TSA is always a circus, but today it was not bad. We got to her domestic gate in A concourse, and the flight was showing on time. They always show up on time until they are late.

We sat down away from other people and held hands. She said, "Dirk, these were a special few days we had together. If I had to make a list of all the things you have shown me... it would be quite a list. I really appreciate you waking up my sexual engine and showing me that I can be sexy. I'll never forget this."

It was my turn to be serious. "Erika, I'll never forget you either. I love the fact that you let me help you with the makeover and helped you get back to enjoying sex. You're a special lady. I really appreciate your advice."

She looked at me with tears in her eyes. "Kiss me once more, then leave and let me sit here quietly, please."

I took her face between my hands and kissed her tenderly. She looked up. "That was like the first kiss. Very sweet."

I stood and looked at her for a moment. She said, "Goodbye, Dirk."

I shook my head. "It's not goodbye, it's I'll see you after a while."

She smiled through her tears. "See you after a while, Dirk."

We looked at each other for a moment longer, then I turned away, heading for the escalator down to the people mover train. I didn't look back, I couldn't stand it if she was still crying, and I might have started crying, too. I mixed in with the crowds trying to get on the train and absent-mindedly got on board with the dozens of people cramming on board. I was oblivious to my surroundings.

Kim? Is that you?

I heard a familiar voice near me. "Hey boomer!"

It was Kim. I was stunned. She was wearing civilian clothes like I was and had a sheaf of paper in her hand. Nearly as tall as I was, with a slim, athletic build, her brown hair pulled into the familiar ponytail, and those flashing green eyes, she looked lovely.

I asked, "What are you doing here?"

"I'm on reserve duty, so I came out to get my schedule and some other paperwork stuff at the operations center. How about you? Getting back from a trip?"

"No, just seeing a friend off."

Kim had come much closer to me in the crowded tram car. "She wears nice perfume, this friend!" she teased.

"Well, we hugged."

Kim laughed. "And maybe kissed? There is a trace of lipstick on your mouth." She reached up with a finger to wipe it away.

The train lurched coming into the T gates, and she stumbled a little. I caught her with one arm while holding the handhold with the other. She was very close to me, and her nose was an inch away from mine. She looked into my soul with those deep green eyes. Her arms went around me, and she held me tight as the train came to a stop.

I kissed her. It seemed like the thing to do. She responded hungrily, our tongues intertwining.

She pulled back, still holding me tight. "I've been waiting for that."

"Me, too. I've been meaning to ask you something, Kim."

She looked at me as the train lurched off towards the terminal. "Yes, Dirk?"

I looked into her eyes. "Would you like to hang out with me and be exclusive boyfriend and girlfriend for the summer? No strings attached. No long-term commitment? Just fun?"

She smiled, and a tear appeared in her pretty eyes. "Yes, Dirk. I'd like that very much."

"Then why are you crying?" I teased.

"Because I'm happy, you dork!"

The train had stopped at the terminal without us realizing it, and all the other passengers had gotten off. "You should let me go. We need to get off."

She shook her head. "I'm never letting go of you."

Kim let go of me long enough for us to get off the train, and we embraced as we rode the escalator up.

"So, this friend you saw off at the airport with the lipstick and nice perfume ... what's that about? Anything I need to be concerned about since I am now promoted to your exclusive girlfriend for the summer?"

I smiled and shook my head. "It's over. Just saying goodbye to a nice lady that helped me with some rough spots while I helped her with some research."

She looked fierce. "It better be over starting right now. I take my rights as exclusive girlfriend very seriously!"

We held hands as we walked to the parking lot.

She asked, "When are you working?"

"Tonight, doing a Rome trip, 1700 show time, back Monday."

She looked at her watch and pondered this. "So... if we head straight back to your condo, we have time for makeup sex before you leave."

I protested. "Were we fighting?"

"Not really. I should be mad at you for not seeing me for a month, but I can be talked out of it. Makeup sex is the best, though. Assuming you are not fucked out from saying goodbye to your friend."

Sometimes there is nothing a guy can say, so it's better to say nothing.

We got to the truck, kissed for a minute, then got in and started towards Norcross and my condo.

She wasn't done. "We'll take a shower first to wash that perfume off you. It's nice, but it ain't mine so it has to go. I want all traces of that woman washed off you before I let you touch me."

"Can I touch you in the shower?" I asked innocently.

"You had damned well better. My solo showers have been incredibly lonely."

I smiled. "I forgot how bossy you are."

"Ah, boomer. You love it and you know it. You've forgotten how adorable I am."

Life with Kim was fast paced and interesting. It was going to be a fun summer.

Don't miss out!

Visit the website below and you can sign up to receive emails whenever Dirk Caldwell publishes a new book. There's no charge and no obligation.

https://books2read.com/r/B-A-UHDZ-RSFMC

BOOKS 2 READ

Connecting independent readers to independent writers.

Did you love *Older Women need Love, too! Erika visits Atlanta*? Then you should read *A Trip to the Lake with Kim*[1] by Dirk Caldwell!

[2]

Airline pilot Dirk meets fellow pilot Kim, and they meet for a long and sensuous vacation at the lake on Dirk's houseboat. You can feel the heat as they explore each other in many ways. The author has supplied exquisite detail that makes the story come to life! Don't miss this latest installment of the series.

Contains:

Consensual sex

Oral Sex

Adult language and situations

---

1. https://books2read.com/u/38WoO7

2. https://books2read.com/u/38WoO7

About the Author

Dirk Caldwell is the pen name of the author of an erotic book series. Dirk embodies the life experiences of the author as an Air Force veteran and commercial airline pilot. Most of the content is true and relates to the author's experiences. It's up to the reader to decide what is fiction and what is true life.